ROLLING THUNDER

Frank and Nancy were preparing to leave the cabin when suddenly he laid a hand on her arm.

"Listen," he said. It was the rumbling sound they'd heard before, but now it was a lot louder and closer.

Nancy ran to the window and looked outside. The rumbling was getting deeper now, shaking the rickety house. Then she saw it—a wall of snow heading down the mountain, right for them!

"It's an avalanche!" Nancy cried.

They ducked beneath the kitchen table as the rumble became a thunderous roar, and then . . .

CRASH!

Nancy Drew & Hardy Boys SuperMysteries

DOUBLE CROSSING
A CRIME FOR CHRISTMAS
SHOCK WAVES
DANGEROUS GAMES
THE LAST RESORT
THE PARIS CONNECTION
BURIED IN TIME
MYSTERY TRAIN
BEST OF ENEMIES

Available from ARCHWAY Paperbacks

A
NANCY DREW & HARDY BOYS Super Mystery™

THE LAST RESORT

Carolyn Keene

AN ARCHWAY PAPERBACK
Published by POCKET BOOKS
New York London Toronto Sydney Tokyo Singapore

This book is a work of fiction. Names, characters, places and incidents are either the product of the author's imagination or are used fictitiously. Any resemblance to actual events or locales or persons, living or dead, is entirely coincidental.

AN ARCHWAY PAPERBACK *Original*

An Archway Paperback published by
POCKET BOOKS, a division of Simon & Schuster Inc.
1230 Avenue of the Americas, New York, NY 10020

Produced by Mega-Books of New York, Inc.

ISBN: 0-671-67461-7

First Archway Paperback printing November 1989

10 9 8 7 6 5 4 3

Printed in the U.S.A.

IL 7+

Chapter One

"IS THIS THE ULTIMATE, or what?" The excitement in her own voice was Bess Marvin's answer. "A week at a gorgeous Colorado ski resort, a chance to see a major music video being made, *and* it's all free—thanks to you, Nancy!"

"Hmmm." Nancy Drew, seated next to Bess, leaned forward in the chair lift, her skis dangling as she surveyed the majestic white world below them. Her reddish blond hair skimmed the padded shoulders of her ski suit. "It certainly looks serene," she murmured.

The resort's lodge and villas were set like jewels around the base of Mount Mirage. Miles of towering snow-covered mountains surrounded the resort and glistened in the winter sun. The complex seemed far removed from the concerns of everyday life, a quality that drew skiers and vacationers from all over the world.

Despite its remoteness, Mount Mirage was busy. The wealthy, the famous, and the powerful used the resort as a retreat and luxury playground.

Ski trails ran down the huge mountain in wide white rivers, converging in a delta near the chalet-style main lodge. Looking down, Nancy watched the flash of brightly dressed skiers weave their way along the trails below.

"I don't get it," George Fayne commented from the other side of Bess. "Why would anyone want to sabotage a place like this?"

"It is hard to believe," Bess said, casually tossing her long blond hair over one shoulder with an easy shrug. "But whatever the problem is, I'm sure Nancy will take care of it."

"I don't know, Bess. Sabotage is very serious," George reminded her, the look in her dark eyes echoing what she'd just said.

Although they were cousins and best friends, two girls couldn't have been less alike than Bess Marvin and George Fayne. Bess was bright and bubbly, while George was thoughtful, quiet, and athletic. Bess's idea of physical exercise was polishing her nails.

"Come on, George," Bess said with a laugh. "Nancy's handled a lot worse cases than this one. I figure we'll knock off the problem in no time. Then we can really enjoy ourselves for the rest of the week!"

Nancy frowned. "I hope you're right, Bess, but something tells me it could be more serious than you think. Apparently, somebody really has it in for this place or its owner." Her blue eyes were focused in the distance. "It couldn't be happening at a worse time, either, considering all the publicity 'High Life' is giving Mount Mirage."

"What a great song," Bess said enthusiastically. "No wonder it's a hit."

"Living the High Life for Love," the song rock star Brad MacDougal had written for Worldwide Children's Charities, was shooting to the top of the charts. The song was being played all over the world as a reminder to help underprivileged kids.

"They're expecting sales of one hundred million!" Bess told her friends. "I read it in a magazine last week."

"It's pretty amazing," George agreed. "But so is the song."

Brad MacDougal performed "High Life" with country singer Roseanne James. They were an unexpected combo—Brad's ripping, rock vocal in harmony with Roseanne's sweet purr—but the blend was magical.

"And to think we'll get to see them making the video right here!" Bess said, a huge grin on her face. The Worldwide Children's Charities had arranged for the song's two stars to make a video at Mount Mirage.

The three girls were almost at the peak. From the lift the skiers below looked like rainbow-colored bits of confetti sprinkled on the sparkling white mountain.

"You know, if I'm not too busy hobnobbing with the rich and famous, I think I just might work on my skiing this week," Bess said. "I saw a couple of incredibly cute instructors at the lodge."

"It probably wouldn't hurt," George said with a laugh. Bess wasn't much of a skier.

"Get ready, we're almost there!" Nancy said as the chair began swinging to a halt.

"Gosh. I don't know where my lip balm is," George muttered, rummaging through the roomy pockets of her silver ski parka. "I could have sworn I put it with my sun goggles."

"Don't worry, I have two," Bess said. She pulled out a small tube of lip gloss. "The last thing I want is dry lips—especially if I get to meet Brad MacDougal. I read that he doesn't have a girlfriend—and you never know."

George shook her head as she pushed up the horizontal bar of the ski lift. "Bess, this is a big place," she said, sliding smoothly onto the snow. "We probably won't even get to see Brad

MacDougal—except maybe on a video monitor."

"Come on, George, think positive!" Bess called after her.

Nancy was the next one off the lift. She pulled down her goggles and held a mittened hand out to Bess. "Here you go," she said, helping her friend slide off.

"Whoa! I just hope I remember how to stop these things," muttered Bess, looking down at her skis. "They seem to have a mind of their own."

"Don't worry, Bess," George assured her. "You'll improve in no time. It's amazing what a cute instructor can do for your technique."

Nancy bent down to check her friend's ski bindings. "With a few pointers, I'll bet you'll be able to take the intermediate trails by the end of the week."

"Me? On the intermediate slopes?" Bess gave Nancy a rueful grin. "Well, thanks for the vote of confidence. But frankly, if I wind up spending a lot of time in the heated pool, or around the fireplace at the lodge, I won't exactly be brokenhearted," Bess said with a giggle. "Picture me and Brad MacDougal curled up in front of a blazing fire. . . ."

George grinned. "Bess, you're hopeless. But at least you *look* like you know what you're doing."

Nancy glanced at Bess's outfit and saw that

George was right. In her white body suit with its high-tech black and red lightning design, Bess Marvin looked like an experienced skier. Only an uneasy wobble in the way she slid along behind George and Nancy gave her away as a beginner.

"I think I'll save the hardest trail until I've had some practice," George said, surveying the trail signs and matching them to the map she'd picked up in the lobby of the lodge. "That would be Excelsior. The next hardest is Zenith. Want to try it, Nancy?"

"Sounds good to me," Nancy said, confident in her ability to handle the trail. In addition to being a natural athlete, Nancy had been introduced to the slopes at a young age. An expert trail like Zenith, or even Excelsior, was perfect for her.

"Well, it's the bunny hill for me," Bess said, pursing her pink-glossed lips. "I don't want to take any chances."

"Don't worry, Bess," Nancy said with a smile. "When Ken Harrison called to invite me here, he told me that the beginner slopes were designed to be accident-proof."

Ken Harrison was a former Olympic silver medalist who owned and operated Mount Mirage. It was he who had asked Nancy and her friends to visit the resort.

"That's comforting," Bess said with a hint of nervousness as she pushed off toward the start of the trails. "Besides, they say whatever goes up must come down—right?"

"Right, but keep it slow," coached George. "Snowplow all the way down if you have to. And whatever you do, don't rush. We'll wait for you by the gondola lift at the base of the mountain, okay?"

"Okay, but I may not get there for years," said Bess, getting a grip on her ski poles. "Let's see if I remember. When I want to stop, I lift my leg and put it out like this, right?" Demonstrating, she nearly lost her balance. Fortunately, Nancy was behind her and put out an arm to brace her friend's back.

"It's easier when you've got a little momentum," Nancy said, patting Bess's shoulder.

"Thanks, Nan," Bess said, blushing. "When I'm laid up in the infirmary with a broken leg, you'll come visit me, right?"

"Come on, we'll go with you to the start of the bunny trail," suggested George. "You'll see how much fun it is. Just don't try anything fancy."

The three girls skied through the light snow over to the approach area just as someone in a white ski suit was inserting the marker that read Bunny.

"Those markers must get knocked over all the time," George commented, as the worker skied off to another approach, a second sign in hand.

"Wait a minute," Nancy exclaimed. She slid a few yards past the start of the trail. "This doesn't look right." A quick look told her that beyond a small clump of trees and some thick bushes, the bunny trail dropped in a headlong plunge.

"They can't expect us beginners to handle something like *that!*" Bess cried, coming up beside Nancy. There was a worried look on her face.

"I don't think so, either, Bess," Nancy murmured, her heart leaping to her throat. "It looks like somebody's changed the trail markers!"

"I think you're right," said George, the snow falling freely now and almost obliterating the map she was consulting. "That's the north face. This trail is definitely an advanced one!"

"No, no, sweetie! Wait for Mommy!" a woman was calling to a small girl who was headed for the far approach of the bunny trail. Out of the corner of her eye, Nancy saw the skier in white planting another trail marker.

"George! Stop them!" she called, pointing to the mother and child. "That child could get killed if they ski that trail!"

"On my way!" George wasted no time in taking off after the pair.

"Bess, stand in the middle over there and warn everyone!" Nancy shouted over her shoulder as she pushed off. The skier in white had just marked another trail. The sign said Easy Street, but it was on the same dangerous face as the bunny slope. Nancy knew this was no "easy" trail.

"Hey," Nancy shouted, trying to stop him or her.

The skier in white didn't even look back before digging in his poles and shoving off down Easy Street.

Nancy wiped her goggles and adjusted her pole straps.

"Wait a minute, Nancy!" Bess called out. "You're not going after that person alone, are you?" she asked.

Nancy's only answer was a *whoosh* as she headed down the sharp drop. After one quick turn, the trail plunged precipitously and disappeared in the swirling snow.

Chapter Two

NANCY WAS IN FOR the ride of her life.

Taking a deep breath, she shot forward. The world dropped out from under her as she sailed off into space. Landing hard, Nancy could feel herself sliding out of control, but with a supreme effort she managed to stop.

But there was no time for a sigh of relief. She stood up and immediately began sliding at top speed. A series of three hairpin turns led into a much narrower trail. Zigzagging for her life, Nancy managed to just remain upright. Her legs grew heavier and heavier as the oxygen was slowly depleted from her body.

Nancy caught a flash of movement ahead. Now she knew the skier in white had nearly a hundred feet on her, but seeing him gave her renewed energy. She leaned into the hill, trying to close the gap.

Every few hundred feet another trail intersected the one she was skiing. Nancy had to keep a close eye on the figure in front of her to make sure he didn't take a cutoff.

Suddenly the treeline broke, and Nancy and her quarry reached a wide-open space, where the blowing snow had calmed to practically nothing. Nancy could see in all directions.

Now was her chance to gain on him. With a few quick turns she had narrowed the distance between them to fifty feet. Then all too soon they were back in the pines, but still skiing at what felt like a million miles an hour.

"Nancy!"

Because of the roaring in her ears, Nancy wasn't sure she had really heard a male voice call out her name.

She turned her head for a split second, and through the pines Nancy did spy another skier racing parallel to her. He was shouting and gesturing wildly with one ski pole.

The momentary distraction made Nancy lose sight of the figure in white. When she looked for him, he had disappeared.

Nancy gasped because in a flash she knew

where the skier had gone. The next moment she shot over the edge of a huge drop and soared in space.

Here goes nothing, Nancy told herself. Lowering her body into a tuck, she used every muscle merely to maintain her equilibrium. After what seemed an eternity, she hit the snow again, hard. She was thrown slightly off balance by the impact but managed to remain upright.

"Nancy!" She heard her name again. This time the voice was closer, and it wasn't one voice, but two.

Nancy shot a quick look to her right. The trees had prevented her from seeing who was calling her name before.

"What?" Skiing along next to her, not more than ten feet away, were Frank and Joe Hardy!

"We're with you!" Nancy heard Joe yell.

With Frank and Joe skiing beside her as lookouts, Nancy could keep her eyes on the skier in front of them.

The trail wound close to the lodge at the mountain's base. More trails and many skiers converged on them as they got closer to the lodge.

Desperately keeping her eyes on her quarry, Nancy dodged the slower skiers who were coming in from their runs. Frank and Joe were sticking right with her, but as the three of them were closing in on their quarry, a ski instructor followed by a group of beginners moved into their path.

Nancy managed to find an opening between two skiers, and Frank and Joe did the same. But when they came out from the group, the figure in white had disappeared!

Nancy slid to a stop. Frank and Joe pulled up next to her, shooting up plumes of snow. Nancy lifted her goggles and narrowed her eyes against the glare of the sun.

"Did you see where he went?" she asked the Hardys in frustration. She looked in the direction of the lodge and the condos behind it.

"Hey, what about saying hello?" Joe Hardy said, smiling.

"Sorry, Joe," Nancy said, adjusting the zipper on her ski suit. "Hey, I didn't know you guys were going to be here!"

"We could say the same about you," Frank Hardy said, looking at her with his warm brown eyes. "Who was that guy anyway, Nancy?"

"Bess, George, and I caught him at the top of the mountain, moving the trail markers," Nancy explained. "Bess almost took an advanced trail."

"Well, it looks like we lost him," Joe said.

Nancy gave Frank and Joe a puzzled look. "This isn't just a lucky coincidence, is it?" she asked.

"Don't tell me Ken called you in, too!" Frank said excitedly.

"Well, I'm not here on vacation, if that's what you mean," Nancy said, returning his slow grin.

Frank's grin grew to include his eyes, and an electric shiver made its way up and down Nancy's spine. Something about Frank Hardy always had this effect on her, though she wasn't sure exactly what it was. It could be his incredible dark eyes, or his easy smile and laugh, or even his patient kindnesses. Or maybe it was his logic and intellect. She couldn't analyze it—now.

Nancy leaned forward on her skis to give first Joe, then Frank a quick kiss hello. "It's great to see you both," she said, trying to sound casual. "Looks like we're partners again."

"Sorry we lost him, Nancy," Frank said seriously. "But I think Ken Harrison should know about this—and soon."

"Lead the way!" Nancy brushed a hair from her half-frozen cheek and followed Frank and Joe to the ski stand in front of the main lodge. They flipped open their bindings and parked their skis on the outdoor racks. "How about George?" Frank asked. "Is she with you?"

"Do you think she'd miss a ski trip?" Nancy asked with a smile.

"Great!" Joe said.

"And Ned?" Frank asked. Ned Nickerson was Nancy's boyfriend. He was handsome, bright, and wonderfully funny—everything a girl could ask for. So why did Nancy's heart skip a beat when she looked at Frank Hardy? It was the craziest thing!

"Ned's studying for midterms," Nancy answered. "But he might be able to come out later in the week," she added quickly.

"So, has Ken told you anything about what's been going on?" Joe asked as they stepped into the lodge.

"No, but Bess, George, and I will meet with him at two o'clock," Nancy said.

"Funny, that's when we're supposed to be meeting Ken, too," Joe said. "But I have a feeling he'll want to see us early."

"Well, here's to working together again," Frank said. Nancy found herself looking forward to this case.

"Welcome to Mount Mirage," Ken Harrison said, walking into the resort's lounge and greeting the three teenagers. Behind his warm smile, Nancy detected the tension he was trying to hide.

Ken's sandy hair was gray at the temples, but he was still as muscular and lean as he'd been sweeping Olympic ski events almost twenty years earlier.

"My office is right in here," he announced,

opening a carved oak door off the lounge with a small key. "Let's talk inside."

Just then Bess and George joined them, and the girls were as surprised as Nancy to see Frank and Joe. The five teenagers followed Ken into a spacious office. A wall of windows on the far side looked out on the slopes.

"Please make yourselves at home," he said, gesturing toward two leather sofas.

As she crossed the room, Nancy saw a group of trophy cases. Her eyes went straight to the central treasures of the collection, three Olympic medals. Ken's career as a competitor had been illustrious, to say the least.

Nancy knew the same couldn't be said for his brief try at acting. Carson Drew had filled his daughter in on Ken's career before Nancy left for Mount Mirage. At the height of his sports fame, Ken had gone to Hollywood and made a few bad films. When the movies failed at the box office, Ken quit the business and opened the resort on Mount Mirage.

There was a gallery of photographs on the wall next to the trophy cases. Most were black-and-white glossies of Ken with celebrity visitors to Mount Mirage: Ken shaking hands with a vice-president; Ken standing next to an Academy Award–winning actor; Ken with a well-dressed man in front of the Mount Mirage condos.

Ken walked over and stood next to Nancy. "That's Jack Treyford, the multimillionaire real estate developer," he explained, observing Nancy's interest in the photo. "He owns some condos here, and he's contributing to the video."

"Gosh, Mr. Harrison, you know so many celebrities!" Bess blurted out from across the room. "Is that Roseanne James?" she asked, pointing to one photo. "I didn't know she played guitar."

Nancy's eyes went to the photograph. It was an eight-by-ten-inch, black-and-white print. Scrawled across the bottom was the message, "All my love, from your biggest fan." There was something haunting in the woman's eyes.

"That isn't Roseanne. It's Jocelyn James, Roseanne's mother, right?" Joe asked.

Ken nodded. "That picture was taken a long time ago."

"They sure look alike," George murmured. "Those eyes . . ."

Ken glanced at the photo tenderly. "She was a beautiful woman, inside and out. We met right after the Olympics twenty years ago. We were hired to do a commercial together, and we—I guess you could say we fell in love."

"What happened?" Nancy asked gently.

Ken shook his head sadly. "It's a long story. But show business can put a real strain on people." He paused. "One day I got a call that she'd killed herself."

"Oh, no! How terrible," Bess said quietly.

"I'm so sorry," Nancy added. "I shouldn't have brought it up."

"You had no way of knowing." Ken's voice wavered a little as he spoke. He coughed to cover his emotions, and then continued. "You know Roseanne will be getting here later today. She's like family to me, and I'd hate to see her involved in the mess I have here. She's had problems enough with her mother dying so young. . . ."

Ken's voice trailed off. He turned away from the others and stared out the wall of windows.

Frank Hardy cleared his throat. "Maybe you'd better start at the beginning, Ken," he suggested quietly. "You mentioned sabotage?"

"Yes, I did. I'm not sure where to begin." Ken turned back and looked at them as if seeing them for the first time. "Let's see. It all started about three months ago. We had an entire shipment of caviar that someone dyed blue. The next week, a rat was let loose in the disco. We caught it the next day, and found the cage it had been brought in, too. After that, one of the gondola lifts got jammed with a strange piece of wire."

Ken picked up a thin, purplish strand from his desk and passed it around the room. Nancy had never seen metal like it before. She handed the strand to Frank, who also looked at it quizzically.

"No one was hurt, but people had to wait for hours while we fixed the lift," Ken continued. "These incidents all sound pretty harmless, but together they can ruin the resort's reputation. And now, with the music video being shot here, Mount Mirage is going to be the focus of a lot of media attention. I want to make sure things go smoothly."

"Unfortunately, whoever did all this is at it again," Nancy told him soberly. She explained about the switched trail markers, adding, "A little girl could have been hurt. Luckily, we were up there."

Ken's face went white. "Oh, no," he murmured. "This is worse than I thought."

"Ken, do you think that the culprit is someone on your staff?" Frank asked.

Ken pursed his lips tensely and nodded. "Well, yes, I've had to think about it. Though honestly, I can't understand why any of them would want to ruin me. I've always been proud of my relationship with the staff. They have unlimited lift passes, competitive salaries . . ."

"It only takes one person with a chip on his or her shoulder, Ken," Nancy observed. Bess nodded.

"You're right. I have to consider that one of them might be behind all this. I did draw up a list of the staff for you." He handed two typewritten pages to Nancy. "It's pretty long, I'm afraid."

Nancy and Frank glanced at the sheets. "This is great," Frank observed. "It even shows what shifts they were assigned to today —that should help us narrow it down."

"If an employee switched those trail markers, he or she either had the time off or sneaked off," Nancy added. "Here, take a look." She handed the list to Joe.

"Whew, this is a lot of alibis to check out," Joe said, scanning the list.

"We'll get started right away," Frank said firmly.

"Wait a minute," George said. "Shouldn't we go undercover to investigate the staff?"

"I'm afraid it's too late for that," Ken replied slowly. "I've let everyone know you were coming. I wanted to scare the culprit." Nancy gave him a curious look, and Ken continued. "I'd like to see this person behind bars—don't get me wrong—but it's even more important to me that nothing happen *this week,* with the video and the documentary and the donors."

"You probably did the right thing," Bess concluded. "If somebody is out to destroy you, now would be the time."

Ken rubbed a hand over his face, then he reached into his jacket pocket. "Here. I've issued you all gold passkeys." He put five shiny keys on his desk and pushed them toward the group.

"What are they for?" Nancy asked, taking hers.

"They open every door in the resort. I'm hoping you won't have to use them, but if you do, you have my full backing. I want these pranks stopped! I love this place. It means the world to me."

A quick knock announced a vivacious woman of about twenty-five who banged the door open and barged into the room. She had dark, blunt-cut hair that framed a pretty and tense face. She marched right up to Ken's desk.

"You've got to come outside right away, Ken," she said in a forceful tone. "My men need to lay their cables, and we're having a problem clearing out the guests!"

Ken put a reassuring hand on the woman's and introduced her. "This is Raven Maxwell, everyone. She's coordinating the video shoot for Archer Lampley, Brad MacDougal's manager and the video's producer. Anything you need to know about the video, ask her."

"Ask me later," Raven interrupted, giving them a none-too-friendly look. "Ken, I need you, and I need you *now.*"

Ken looked at them helplessly. "Why don't you get started on that list. I'll check in with you later."

"We're on our way." Frank nodded, and in no time they were out in the lounge planning their attack.

"Whew!" Joe commented. "I'd never want to work for her!"

Frank nodded. "I think we should get started. Nancy and George, would one of you show me where you saw that person switching the trail markers?"

"I've got an idea," Nancy said. "Why don't you and Joe go back with George up the mountain, and Bess and I will start checking out the staff here in the lodge."

"Good idea," Bess said. She pointed to a tear in the side of her ski suit. "I ran into a tree on the way down the mountain. Maybe I can find a new suit in one of the boutiques while we're at it."

"We're here to work, Bess, not shop," Nancy chided her.

"Just trying to mix business with pleasure," Bess retorted, her blue eyes sparkling mischievously.

"We'll leave you two to settle this," Frank said with a smile. "See you later."

"Later," Nancy replied, feeling a vague regret that she wasn't going with them.

She shook it off as she and Bess headed down the corridor toward Snazz, the boutique located next to the magazine concession.

"I saw this electric-blue suit with white

stripes in the window. I think it'd look great on me," Bess said. "What if I try it on while you check out the staff?"

"Oh, all right," Nancy agreed.

Inside the store, the air was perfumed with a rich, pleasant scent. "May I help you?" a well-dressed saleswoman asked.

"Yes, I'd like to try on the blue suit in the window, please," Bess told her.

"I'll wait here," Nancy said. The saleswoman brought the suit to Bess, and Nancy pretended to browse as her friend went into the changing room.

Nancy was examining an orange sweater, watching the sales staff out of the corner of her eye, when she heard a noise from the changing room. It sounded like Bess. She was coughing—once, twice, then repeatedly.

"Bess, are you all right?" Nancy asked, knocking on the door. There was no answer.

Nancy put her hand on the door and was about to open it when she realized it was burning hot. She looked down at the floor and saw a white plume drifting up from the base of the door. And from behind the door came the smell of thick, acrid smoke!

Chapter Three

COVERING HER MOUTH, Nancy pushed on the door. It wouldn't budge. Leaning into it with her shoulder, Nancy shoved in and up with everything she had. The door moved six inches and then stopped. Nancy slid in and found the reason the door wouldn't open. Bess. She was lying on the floor, overcome by the smoke. It clutched at Nancy's throat and choked her now, too.

Nancy lifted her friend under the arms and dragged Bess out of the changing room. Away from the smoke, Bess revived somewhat. She managed to get to her feet and stagger into the corridor.

Nancy turned to the salesperson and customers. "Get out of here right away!" she shouted. "There's a fire!"

The saleswoman looked startled as Nancy tugged at her sleeve. "Cover your mouth," Nancy ordered, pushing her to the safety of the corridor. "Now run for it!

"Please find the nearest exit and get out!" Nancy announced, urging everyone into the corridor. She turned back to Bess. "Are you all right?"

Bess's eyes were streaming, and she was still coughing. "I think so," she managed to say. "The door was stuck, and the room just filled up with smoke. Where are you going?" she added, grabbing Nancy's arm as her friend headed for the smokiest part of the building.

"I'll see you outside," Nancy answered. A general murmur of alarm was running through the lodge now. People were pouring out of the exits.

"What do you mean?" Bess demanded, still holding on to her friend's arm. "Aren't you coming out?"

"I have to check something first. Now go!" Nancy insisted.

"I can't leave you in a burning building!" Bess cried.

"I'll be all right, Bess. I promise."

"If I didn't know how stubborn you were, Nancy Drew . . ." Bess muttered. With a final glance back, she hurried toward the nearest exit along with the others.

Nancy covered her nose and throat with a handkerchief and squinted up at the ceiling in the hallway. The smoke was coming from the ceiling beams, which were made of dark-stained wood. They appeared to be more decorative than functional, and looking closely, Nancy saw that they had metal vents spaced at regular intervals.

The beams probably disguised the central air system, Nancy reasoned. Following her hunch, she turned down an empty corridor, keeping her head as low as she could and breathing in shallow gasps.

The beams ended just outside the swinging doors of the kitchen. Just inside the doors, she found another door, this one marked Authorized Personnel Only.

Nancy pushed that door open and was nearly overpowered by the smoke. She lifted her sweater over her mouth and nose to help block it out. These makeshift masks worked, but she knew they were only temporary measures. If she was going to get anything done, she'd have to work fast.

Through tearing eyes, Nancy made out a flight of stairs going down. She fought her way through the smoke to the bottom.

The central air system was across the room.

Just in front of it, someone had built a bonfire. Flames were roaring by the air-intake fan.

Nancy fought her way back up the stairs to the kitchen and grabbed a fire extinguisher. Then she ran back down to the generator room and pressed the silver lever on the extinguisher. A stream of white mist shot out, and in less than a minute the fire was under control.

A few more blasts and the fire was completely extinguished. Coughing furiously from the smoke she'd inhaled, Nancy dragged herself back up the stairs.

As she made her way back through the deserted corridors, she heard the distant wail of a fire siren. When she reached the main exit, Ken Harrison rushed up to her, Bess right behind him.

"Nancy! What happened?" Ken's face was flushed, and his pale blue eyes were wide with alarm.

"Are you all right?" Bess asked.

"I'll be fine." Nancy leaned against the wall while she caught her breath. "It was a fire, all right. Someone had built a bonfire in front of the intake fan. Definitely not an accident." Her words came out in short gasps.

"Good grief," Ken said, rubbing his jaw nervously. "This is just what I need! The whole place smells of smoke, and everyone's terrified. Are *you* okay?"

"Just a little tired," Nancy answered, beginning to recover from her ordeal. "Anyhow, the fire's out now."

"You say the fire's out? Why, then, little lady, what you need is my help." A surprisingly cheerful man dressed in a houndstooth business jacket with a turquoise string tie came up to them. The woman with him wore a zebra-striped ski suit.

"Chester, darling," she was saying in a distinctly western twang, "how's the man going to accept our help when he doesn't even know who we are?"

"Why then, allow me to introduce myself," said the little man, with a tip of his beige ten-gallon hat. "I'm Chester L. Peabody, and this here is my wife, Pearl. We're from Jobbo, Texas, a little town I suspect none of you has ever heard of. Am I right?"

Nancy couldn't help smiling as she nodded. As for Bess and Ken, they seemed too surprised to speak. The fire siren still sounded in the distance, but no engines had appeared yet.

"He's an inventor," Pearl explained proudly. "He's got patents on fifteen inventions already, with over forty pending."

"And one of those inventions gets rid of odors entirely. Why, I'll have that smoke smell out of here in fifteen minutes or less. Just lead me to the source of the fire."

"By all means," Ken said, obviously willing

to try anything. He nodded to Nancy, who simply raised her eyebrows quizzically and led them back into the building.

"Just three years ago, I had only a workshop in my garage," Chester announced.

"Now he's got his own lab with five employees," his wife added with pride. "And all because he played our anniversary-date numbers and my birthdate."

"I told her when I married her that she'd bring me luck," Chester added. "It just took me some twenty years. I won a million dollars for every year we were married!"

"You won twenty million dollars in a lottery?" Nancy said.

"Sure did." The little man chuckled.

As they pushed through the service door and made their way down the stairs, Ken threw Nancy a helpless shrug and a smile that seemed to say Chester L. Peabody might seem like an eccentric, but he might also be able to help. Stranger things had been known to happen.

"Oh, I see," Chester murmured, walking up to the charred remains of the bonfire, looking from it to the blower, which was still on. "That blower goes through the whole lodge, right?"

"Right," Ken answered glumly.

"Hmmm. Well, let's see, then . . ." Reaching into his pocket, Chester took out two small vials.

"It'll take a tad of this," he murmured, taking a pinch of green powder from one and adding it to the other. "Now, where are the controls for your blower?"

"The switch is over here," Ken said, pointing to the wall. "Should I turn it off?"

"Just for a minute," Chester instructed.

Chester lightly flicked some powder into the engine. "Okay," he said, "turn her on again."

The huge generator rumbled into action.

"That should do it," Chester announced, carefully capping the tubes and inserting them in his jacket pocket. "Don't worry. This stuff won't harm the motor. It'll be gone without a trace in fifteen minutes."

"Well, if you've fixed it, let's go," Pearl said. "This room is no place to spend a vacation."

As soon as they stepped back into the corridor, Bess sniffed the air. "It's already fresher. Amazing," she commented.

Instead of reeking of stale smoke, the air coming through the kitchen vent was as sweet as the air on Mount Mirage.

"I'll say," a grateful Ken agreed. "Mr. Peabody—how can I thank you?"

"No thanks required," Chester said. "I'm glad to help. Just one thing: please don't mention this to anyone," he said in a conspiratorial whisper. "I haven't registered the formula yet. In fact, that's the reason I had it with me. Never leaves me—afraid of somebody stealing it."

"Don't worry, your secret's safe with us," Nancy said with a smile.

"Well, 'bye now, folks. I'm going to the pool. Coming, Chester?" Pearl asked.

"Sure thing, honey." With a tip of his hat, the little man followed his wife down the corridor.

"I can't believe what a good job that stuff did," Ken commented. "We're lucky they came along." Just then they heard the fire engines pull up outside.

Unlike Ken, Nancy wasn't terribly relieved. Someone had started that fire, intending to do more than cause a bit of smoke. The acts of sabotage were getting more serious.

"We'd have been sunk without Chester and Pearl," Ken went on. "I'd better go out and greet the fire fighters. Oh, by the way, Roseanne and Brad will be here later. They're starting the taping tonight."

"I don't know about you, but my head is spinning," Bess said. "I need a nap if I'm going to be awake tonight."

"Good idea," Ken said, a look of concern in his eyes. "You *both* look like you could use some sleep."

"But Frank and Joe—" Nancy began.

"Frank and Joe can take care of themselves," Bess said, overriding her. "At the least, you should take a shower—the air may be clean, but I can't say the same for us!"

"Okay," Nancy agreed reluctantly.

They waved a quick goodbye to Ken, who still looked terribly worried.

"We'll get to the bottom of this," Nancy said, trying to reassure him. But she had a feeling it wasn't going to be easy.

That evening, Nancy arrived at the disco feeling clean and refreshed after a shower, a nap, and some dinner. Bess, George, and the Hardys were changing and planned to meet her there for the first night of videotaping. Ken Harrison had requested that they keep an eye on the stars and crew. It was most important that the taping run smoothly.

Nancy was surprised to see a sign on the door of the disco that read Soundstage. "We converted it for the week," said Raven Maxwell, whizzing by her. She seemed to have read Nancy's mind. "Ken told me who you are, by the way. Make yourself at home, but try not to get in the way, okay?"

Nancy looked around for a place to stand, but found she was in the way no matter where she went. Finally she backed into the DJ's booth, which was serving as the control center. Raven was shouting into a microphone for someone to move something, and technicians were fiddling with all sorts of camera equipment.

"Well, hello! Are you our new engineer?" The voice behind her had a rough, earthy quality. Nancy recognized it immediately, as would have millions of other girls. She spun around and found herself looking into the fabulous, clear blue eyes of Brad MacDougal.

"Sorry, I'm just an observer. You're Brad MacDougal, right?" she asked, shaking the hand he offered and returning his broad smile.

"Yep," Brad said modestly. "What's your name?"

"Nancy Drew," she answered.

He looked at her with new interest. "Whoa! I heard about you!" he said, his smile widening. "You're the one who saved the guy from Bent Fender! And didn't you have something to do with helping Jesse Slade out of a pretty bad jam?"

Nancy nodded.

"I'm a fan, Nancy. You're terrific!"

Nancy had to laugh. "This is supposed to be the other way around," she said, shaking her head. "Shouldn't I be saying I'm *your* fan?"

"Not unless you really are," he replied, batting his long lashes dramatically.

"Well, I am, actually," Nancy said with a smile. "And I love 'Living the High Life.' You and Roseanne are wonderful together!"

"Thanks," Brad answered, looking genuinely pleased. "That's the first nice thing I've heard all day."

"Oh?" Nancy smiled encouragingly. After all, she thought, she was at Mount Mirage to pick up information, and what better source than the star of the video himself? "Has it been rough?"

"Rough is not the word," Brad said with a scowl. "Archer Lampley, the producer and my manager, has been his usual self—" He caught himself. "Oh, well, you don't want to hear all my problems."

Nancy was about to explain that actually she did want to hear his problems, when Raven Maxwell burst into the control booth. "Get this, Brad." Raven whispered something in Brad's ear. "Not only that," she concluded in her regular voice, "but he was proud of it, too. Isn't that incredible?"

"It sure is," Brad muttered. Whatever Raven had said, it had an intense effect on the singer. His face was beet red, and his hands were now balled into fists. Nancy couldn't believe how fast his mood had changed.

"I'm going to have to talk to him," Brad said, storming out of the control room.

Through the glass door, Nancy watched him approach a man in a conservative business suit, who she guessed was probably one of the studio executives. Slipping out of the control booth, Nancy followed Brad at a discreet distance.

"You think you can do anything, Archer Lampley! Just because you're a big-shot producer," Brad was saying in an angry voice.

As Brad was speaking, Frank and Joe walked in. But like Nancy and everybody else in the room, they stopped in their tracks as the rock star's shouts escalated.

"You know what you really are, Archer? You're a piece of garbage!" he shouted through gritted teeth. "You don't deserve to live!"

Nancy's jaw fell open as Brad leapt at the producer. Before anyone could stop him, the singer had his hands around Lampley's throat—and was squeezing as hard as he could!

Chapter Four

FRANK AND JOE raced up to the rock star and the producer. Nancy met them there. With lightning speed, Joe wrenched Brad's hands away from Lampley.

"Okay, calm down," Joe murmured to Brad, who was panting hard.

"Listen to Joe, Brad," Nancy added, stepping between Brad and Archer. "Whatever you're upset about, attacking Lampley isn't going to help."

Brad shot them a look that was half regretful, half grateful. "I guess you're right," he admitted. "But he deserves to be killed, I swear—" His eyes burning with hatred, Brad glared over at Lampley, who was standing with Frank.

Looking unruffled, Archer Lampley nevertheless was sticking close to Frank. "The kid's got some sense of gratitude," he said sarcastically. "When I first met him, he was playing in a tiny club for peanuts. I made him a superstar, and now he wants to kill me!"

Nancy was impressed by how calmly the crew seemed to be taking everything. With scarcely a glance in Brad and Archer's direction, they finished up their work, setting up microphones and laying down cables.

"I just wanted to remind you that I have witnesses to your little performance," Lampley told Brad with a sneer. "Witnesses, do you hear?" With a smug look he pointed to Nancy, Joe, and Frank. Then he waved a finger around the room at the other technicians.

Brad shook his head incredulously. "You're an idiot, Archer, you know that? I wouldn't even mind you being an idiot, if you weren't a rotten thief, too. So just leave me alone, okay?"

"Take it easy," Joe said, patting the singer gently on the back.

With a final disgusted look at Lampley, Brad walked away.

"An ingrate. An utter ingrate," Lampley was muttering to no one in particular. Then, when Raven walked by, he announced, "I'm leaving.

I'll be back, however, and I expect a full rehearsal before Roseanne gets here. Make sure he does it." Lampley pointed a sharp finger in Brad's direction.

"Of course, Archer," Raven answered dryly.

Lampley nodded to Nancy, Frank, and Joe, and then strode out of the room, rubbing his throat.

"You're certainly taking all this in stride," Joe told Raven, who was smiling slightly.

Raven laughed. "Oh, we're used to outbursts like that around here," she said.

"You are?" Nancy asked. She exchanged a look with Frank and Joe.

Raven shrugged. "When you work with Archer Lampley, you hear them all the time. Everyone in the entire world hates Archer—everyone who knows him, that is."

"Really?" Frank asked. "Why?"

Raven laughed again. "Why hate Archer? I suppose if you ask each person who hates him, you'll get a different story."

"Let's start with Brad, then," Nancy said coolly, her eyes meeting Raven's.

Raven quickly scanned the room. "Okay. Ken told me to be upfront with you. Let's sit down over there so we'll be out of the crew's way while they finish up." She pointed to a small table. "Brad will need a few minutes to pull himself together, anyway."

She addressed a crew member. "We'll rehearse in five." The assistant nodded and hurried off.

"Now, about Brad and Archer," Raven began after she and the three detectives were sitting down. "For starters, there are the finances. Archer was able to sign Brad on when Brad was a nobody. The contract is great for Archer, but lousy for Brad. For the rest of his life, Brad MacDougal has to pay Archer Lampley forty percent of everything he makes. Not only that, Archer owns most of Brad's songs outright."

Joe whistled softly. "Whew. Forty percent, that's pretty incredible."

"Let's put it this way, it was a stunning move on Archer's part. And naturally, Brad resents it." Raven tapped her manicured fingers on the table. "But *c'est la vie.* Business is business. Archer simply made a good deal for himself."

"Is that what this fight was all about?" Nancy asked. She wasn't sure if she trusted Raven. After all, something Raven told Brad had inspired him to attack Lampley.

"Well, in a way," Raven said, looking away. She paused, then turned back to Nancy. "Actually, I caused the fight," she admitted with a shake of her head. "I told Brad something he had no business knowing."

"Oh?" Frank leaned in and listened closely.

"You see, poor Brad was under the impression that all the money Archer's getting for

'High Life' is going to World Children's Charities." She raised her eyebrows and shook her head gently.

"You mean it isn't?" Joe said.

"Of course not. Archer Lampley Productions is strictly for profit. Archer's making a fortune on all this. World Children's Charities is getting only a small percentage. A very small percentage."

Raven explained everything as if it were all perfectly normal, but Nancy could hardly believe what she was hearing.

"But Brad had trusted him?" Frank asked.

Raven nodded. "Archer apparently promised to turn his cut over to the charity if Brad would record with Roseanne. That's why he was able to produce the double vocal on 'High Life.' Roseanne's another of his clients, just as her mother was. That means Archer will collect double commissions."

"Why did you tell him the truth now?" Nancy asked Raven.

"Oh, I know I shouldn't have," Raven said. "It's just that Archer was bragging about the whole arrangement at dinner, and—I don't know—I knew Brad would find out eventually, so I decided sooner was better than later."

"Raven, where do you stand on all this?" Frank asked directly. Nancy smiled to herself—trust Frank to get right to the point.

"Well, it's complicated," Raven answered

with a shrug. "I do wish WCC were getting the whole bundle. But on the other hand, I admire Archer tremendously. I've worked with him for five years, and I've learned everything there is to know about producing and promoting from him. The man's a genius at making money. What more could you want in a music promoter?"

Raven seemed about to say more, but a burly crew member interrupted her. "Raven, where do you want these lights?" he asked.

"Sorry to cut this short, but I'd better go mind the store," Raven said, standing up and checking her Lucite clipboard. "Over by those receivers," she called out. With a nod and a smile, she walked away from Nancy, Joe, and Frank.

"Let's go, everyone! Let's go!" Raven barked loudly. "We've got just enough time for a rehearsal before Roseanne gets here."

"What did we miss? Anything?" Nancy spun around to see a bubbly Bess looking down at her, her face full of happy anticipation. George was right behind her, looking equally excited.

"Oh, nothing much," Frank answered for Nancy. "Just a murder attempt."

"What?" Bess sputtered.

"Brad attacked Archer Lampley," Nancy explained.

"Why?" George asked.

"It's all over now. I'll fill you in later. Brad's

in the control room getting ready for a rehearsal, and Roseanne's due any minute. Grab a seat." Nancy pointed to two chairs from the next table.

Bess pulled the chairs over and turned to George. "You see, George, we are going to get to see Brad MacDougal in action. I hope I don't faint!"

The others shot one another amused looks as Bess stared at the stage in utter fascination. She didn't have long to wait. In a few moments Brad MacDougal took his place under the lights.

"I want to see some real vulnerability here, Brad," the director was urging from his place next to the cameraman. Brad snorted in response, but sat down at the bistro table set up on stage. On it was a slender vase with a single red rose.

"Take one, Brad alone in the bistro," said a young woman with a black-and-white film clapboard.

"Can you believe this?" Bess whispered excitedly.

"Run the intro for him," Raven barked from the control booth.

The familiar slow beat of "Living the High Life for Love" began, and a sense of exhilaration coursed through the room. Alone, on stage, acting out the part of a lonely lover, Brad looked as if he had forgotten his other troubles. He leaned forward, his eyes troubled and sad as he hummed the first note that started the vocal.

"He's so gorgeous," Bess murmured.

As Brad launched into the song, Nancy was aware that someone had just entered the room. Craning her neck, she watched as Roseanne James, the undisputed queen of country rock, appeared among the crew.

Brad sang the first refrain of the song as everyone listened, spellbound. Then he turned to the director. "Vulnerable enough for you?" he asked with a smile.

"Hello, everybody!" Roseanne called out.

"Hi, Roseanne," a chorus went up from around the room. Brad blew a kiss from the stage.

"Two minutes, everyone, while we get Roseanne set up," Raven announced.

"Welcome to Mount Mirage, Roseanne." Brad ambled down from the platform to greet his costar. The two were standing close enough to Nancy's table that she and her friends could hear every word.

"One of the stagehands told me you and Archer had a little run-in," Roseanne said to Brad with a smile.

"He lied about his percentage," Brad told her. "He's not giving all the money to WCC. That was just a ploy to get us to record."

Roseanne pursed her pretty lips and gave a

hard smile. "It's okay, Brad. He's going to get his back. I have it on very good information that Archer Lampley is not long for this world."

"Are you serious?" Brad asked.

"Totally," Roseanne replied, the same hard smile on her lips. "Because *I'm* going to kill him."

She made the threat so calmly that Nancy didn't know what to think. George's mouth had dropped open. Bess's eyes were huge, and Frank and Joe shot each other confused looks.

"What did I tell you?" Raven whispered in Nancy's ear as she passed by. "Somebody's always got it in for Archer. Never means a thing.

"Bring the boom mike up here," Raven added, speaking to a crew member.

"Yes, I am going to kill him," Roseanne repeated calmly. "Unless you beat me to it, that is."

Suddenly Brad and his costar burst out laughing. Nancy relaxed—obviously, this was a way they let off steam. Still, these casual references to murder were unsettling.

"I am kidding, of course," Roseanne said.

A man with a boom mike maneuvered past the table where the kids were sitting. As he reached Roseanne, the boom suddenly slid out of his grasp. It collided with the country singer, knocking her purse to the floor.

The bag skidded away, coming to rest at Joe's feet.

"I'll get it!" Roseanne cried sharply. She lunged for the bag and grabbed it out of Joe's hand.

Roseanne's movements were quick but not fast enough to hide a small, pearl-handled revolver sticking out of the corner of the bag!

Chapter Five

As Nancy watched, Joe Hardy calmly tucked the small revolver back into the bag and handed it to Roseanne.

"Thank you," the singer murmured softly.

"Anytime," Joe replied, with a confused look in his eye. Roseanne gave him a tense smile before turning away.

Before Nancy could say anything to her friends about what had just happened, Raven was walking across the room to check out possible damage to the boom mike.

"Are you okay?" she asked the singer, almost as an afterthought.

"Oh, I'm fine," Roseanne said quickly, with a frown. "But I am tired. Tell Archer I'll report to work early tomorrow morning. I need a little time to rest if I'm going to do this well."

"Archer's not going to like it, but suit yourself," Raven told Roseanne with a shrug. Raven pushed her pencil back behind her ear and sighed exasperatedly. Turning to the crew, she announced, "No shoot today, folks. I'll post call times for tomorrow on the door."

As Roseanne hurried across the room, Joe looked over at his brother and Nancy. Frank raised his eyebrows at Nancy, then pointed to Joe. "Go for it," Nancy said.

"You're on," Frank said to Joe, indicating the departing Roseanne.

Joe stood up with a smile. "Now, this is the kind of assignment I enjoy. Thanks, partners."

In an instant he was at the exit, holding the door open for the pretty singer.

"Oh! Thank you again," Nancy heard her say before the two disappeared into the corridor.

"Joe'll fill us in later," Frank said. "As for me, I'm going to head back to my room. I want to go over the employee list Ken gave us. Breakfast at nine?" he suggested. "That'll give us time to get a little work done in the morning, too."

Nancy nodded. She couldn't help admiring the fact that until a case was solved, Frank never stopped working. That kind of total immersion had a way of paying off.

"Can I walk you to your room?" he asked Nancy and her friends. Frank and Joe were staying in one wing of the lodge, and Nancy and her friends were on the other side.

"No thanks, Frank," Nancy answered for all of them. "We'll be fine."

"See you tomorrow, then," he said, holding the door open.

"Tomorrow," Nancy agreed, as she watched him make his way down the corridor. A familiar feeling came over her. Seeing too much of Frank Hardy always seemed to prove dangerous.

Joe Hardy walked beside a silent Roseanne James. "Can I ask you a personal question?" he asked finally.

"That depends on what you want to know," she answered guardedly.

"Do you always carry a gun with you?"

Roseanne looked down at the carpet, and a shadow crossed her face. "Here we are. This is my room," she said, fishing through her bag for the key to her suite.

"You haven't answered my question," Joe said softly.

"That's true," she said with a sigh. "Do I

always carry a gun? The answer is yes. Always. Now, good night."

Joe didn't move as she put her key in the door, then turned it. "I said good night. And thanks for your help."

The strain of the past few minutes was beginning to show, and Joe couldn't help feeling sorry for the pretty singer. Nevertheless, he pressed on.

"You're not telling me the whole truth, are you?" He tried to keep his voice soft and gentle.

Roseanne snapped, "I'm not obligated to discuss any of this with you." Then, responding to the look of genuine concern on his face, she softened. "Well, okay. The truth is, I *don't* always carry a gun."

Her wide-set, deep brown eyes searched his intently, as if deciding whether she could trust him. He smiled reassuringly, and she continued. "I got the gun because I started getting threatening fan mail. It scared me. You know, some people out there are really crazy," she explained softly.

"Have you gone to the police about it?" Joe asked her, staring hard into her eyes.

"Oh, no," Roseanne said, shaking her head. "I don't want to get the police involved. For all I know, the letters may be nothing more than pranks. But still, I didn't want to take any chances."

"So you carry a gun? I'm not sure I follow your logic, but it's your decision," Joe said. "Just don't go dropping it on the floor in front of a room full of people again, okay?" He added, "Especially when you've been joking about murder."

Roseanne blushed. "That was stupid. I'll be careful from now on, I promise."

When she smiled at him, Joe felt a warm rush go through him. "If you need anything," he said, almost stumbling over the words, "my name's Joe Hardy."

"Thank you, Joe. I know who you are. Ken filled me in. I might just take you up on it," she replied. "Well, good night. And thanks again."

"Good night," he murmured.

With another smile and a fluttery wave, she let herself into her room. Joe sighed. Roseanne James was charming enough to make him believe every word she'd said, but his instincts told him that she was hiding something.

Hurrying back to the room he shared with Frank, he found his brother getting ready for bed. He thought about talking to him but decided to let it wait until morning. He'd find out what Roseanne James was afraid of soon enough.

Next morning, at a late breakfast, Nancy and her friends were seated around a large glass table in the lodge's elegant Skylight Room.

"Everything hurts!" Bess cried. "And to think all I did was go down the bunny slope that one time!"

"I don't know about you, but I'm definitely going to put in a lot of time on the slopes today," George said. "I ran into Ken on my way here, and he said he'd let me borrow his custom-made skis. We're about the same height, so they should do. I can't wait!" George took a bite of her rich almond croissant.

Bess turned her eyes away and concentrated on her low-calorie cereal. But she couldn't resist saying, "How come you can eat stuff like that and never gain weight?"

"Exercise," said George with a sly wink.

"Here's Frank," Nancy interrupted. She watched the older Hardy brother thread his way over to their table.

"Morning, everyone," Frank said, pulling out a chair for himself. "Joe's on his way."

"What happened with Roseanne?" Nancy asked eagerly.

"Not much, apparently. But I'll let him tell you," Frank said, helping himself to some juice.

A few minutes later Joe arrived. "So?" Nancy asked. "Did Roseanne tell you why she was carrying a gun?"

"For protection. Or so she said," Joe answered. "According to her, she's been getting some pretty ugly fan mail lately, and she's scared."

"Wow." Bess shuddered. "The price of fame—"

"I think it's pretty strange to bring a gun to a charity event," George murmured.

"Not if you think your life is in danger!" Joe said, speaking up in Roseanne's defense. From the ardor in his voice, Nancy could tell he'd been more than a little affected by the star.

"Well, I did a little homework," Frank said. "I managed to narrow down the lists Ken gave us to twenty-three people unaccounted for at the time the markers were changed."

"Only twenty-three, huh?" George said, with a wry smile. "It's a good thing there are five of us."

"How should we divvy it up?" Bess asked.

"I think we should concentrate on the people who work outdoors and study them first, if possible," Nancy suggested. "The person who changed those markers was a really good skier."

"That would be ski instructors and some of the maintenance crew. I guess we should check out the medics, too," Frank replied.

"What about the people who work at that coffee shop on the top of the mountain?"

George threw in. "They may not all be great skiers, but they were right up there when the markers got changed."

"Right. I have their names here. Well, that adds five more people to the list," Frank said.

"I think I should hang around while they're shooting the video," Joe said.

Frank shot his brother a quizzical look but nodded in agreement. "Someone ought to, and Roseanne trusts you."

Nancy pushed her cup of tea away and leaned across the table. "Okay, then. Here's the plan. Joe keeps an eye on Roseanne. Bess can check out the indoor staff." Bess smiled gratefully. "George, Frank, and I will cover the slopes. I think we should ski as much as possible. That way, if anybody's been tampering with the runs, we'll find out about it."

"Good thinking, Nancy." Frank grinned warmly at her as he folded his papers and returned them to his pocket. "What do you say we wrap up this case by tomorrow?"

"That would be fantastic. I could use a few days at Mount Mirage—on the slopes, in the sauna, at the disco," Nancy said, smiling back. There was that feeling again. Frank's eyes were like two magnets that she couldn't resist!

"Ahem," George said, wiping her mouth delicately with a linen napkin. "Are we ready?"

"I'm ready," Nancy said, grateful that none of her friends could tell that her heart was beating double time. "Let's go." She stood up, all business.

Still, when they walked away from the table, she couldn't help staring at Frank again. He was so smart and so competent. Now stop it! Nancy chided herself as the group walked toward the exit. She had a boyfriend, and Frank had a girlfriend, and that was that.

The crisp mountain air brought Nancy back to the case. Whoever was jeopardizing people at Mount Mirage had to be stopped. Snapping on her skis and gliding over to the lift with the others, she took her place across from George. The mechanism purred into action, lifting them into the air.

Looking out at the majestic mountains around her, Nancy let her mind drift. There was a challenge in that sparkling white world. Ken Harrison, who loved this mountain more than anything, was being driven off it. Why? And by whom?

"That's strange," George said. "Look at that building on the lower slope, behind those trees. It really looks out of place, doesn't it?"

Nancy looked down. The building George was pointing to was an old wooden structure. Unlike the rest of the modern complex, it was small, old, and run-down.

"It looks like a shed," Frank said as he peered down. "But I suppose we should find out exactly what it is. You never know."

Good old thorough Frank, Nancy thought.

When they stepped off the lift, Nancy, Frank, and George headed over to the lift operator, a young woman wearing a jacket with the double *M* logo of Mount Mirage.

"Hi," Nancy said. "We were wondering about a building we saw from the lift. About halfway down the mountain, under a kind of cliff," she explained.

"Oh, you must mean Pete Dawson's house," the operator said as she set the lift back in motion. "It was part of the mines that were here before the resort was built. Pete's right over there, if you want to talk to him." The operator pointed to a wiry man with scraggly reddish blond hair. He was bolting in new trail markers.

"Let's go," Frank said, gliding over. Nancy and George followed.

"Pete Dawson?" The man looked at Frank suspiciously. "Yeah. That's me," he said. "You're the detectives, aren't you?"

"That's us," Nancy admitted. Before she could continue, Dawson shrugged and turned away.

"Don't look at me," he muttered. "I don't know the first thing about it."

"About what?" Nancy asked, puzzled.

"About the lift being jammed! I wasn't even on duty that morning." He glared at them, then turned and glided over to the next trail marker. Obviously, as far as Pete Dawson was concerned, the conversation was over.

"What's eating him?" Frank murmured.

"He is irritable, isn't he?" George remarked with a shrug of her shoulders.

"This is absolutely unacceptable!" The petulant voice of someone scolding the lift operator stopped Nancy from commenting. She spun around to see a middle-aged man tapping his ski pole into the snow. A heavy gold chain around his wrist glinted in the morning sun. "That patch is pure ice! Where's the snow machine? You people are supposed to maintain these slopes!"

"I'm sorry, Mr. Treyford," the operator apologized.

Treyford. He had to be Jack Treyford, Nancy realized, the multimillionaire real estate entrepreneur Ken had mentioned.

Staring at him, she realized why he looked so familiar. Treyford's photo had been in every newspaper and magazine lately, publicizing his autobiography. His organization was behind some enormous construction projects, and he owned a chain of super-luxury hotels.

"If I owned this place, the staff would spread

fresh powder out here every morning," Treyford said. "It costs a little more, but it's the only way to run a world-class ski resort!"

"Well, folks, if you don't mind," George said, turning to Frank and Nancy, "it's time for me to do a little investigating of my own. On Excelsior," she explained with a grin.

"Good luck," Nancy told her.

"Young lady!" Treyford called, seeing George glide to the approach. "I suggest you watch out for that ice patch there! It's about two feet wide."

George turned and raised an eyebrow. Nancy knew that a small patch of ice like the one he described would never disturb George's skiing, but George acknowledged the warning politely. "Thanks, I'll be careful."

"There should be a marker there. Unfortunately, the man who runs this place doesn't know how to maintain it properly." Treyford stormed off.

Nancy remembered that Treyford's hotel chain was known for its many luxuries—and its high rates. Every other place in the whole world must seem like a comedown to him, Nancy thought.

"Well, guys. Ken's skis feel great!" George called, pushing away from Frank and Nancy toward the expert run. "See you on the south face!"

"Okay, George," Nancy called out. She watched her friend move onto the trail, taking the first drop with dazzling ease.

"I love watching her ski," Nancy murmured to Frank in admiration.

"I know," Frank agreed. "She's really good."

Suddenly Nancy gasped. Ten feet down the slope George made a sharp turn to avoid Treyford's patch of ice. But as she leaned into the mountain, one of her skis snapped in two!

As her friends looked on in horror, George tumbled head over heels down the slope, completely out of control!

Chapter Six

"COME ON!" Nancy shouted. She and Frank pushed off after George. A short way down the slope, they found part of the broken ski. Frank skidded to a stop to pick it up, but Nancy skied on to where her friend had fallen.

Nancy found George half buried in a drift of soft snow about a quarter of a way down the trail.

"George? George?" She called out her friend's name as she frantically scooped the snow off her.

"Nan?" George's voice was weak, and Nancy saw that her face was tight with pain. "I think my wrist is broken." She groaned softly, tears slipping from the corners of her eyes.

"Oh, George." Nancy helped her friend sit up. "Are you sure that's all? I mean, you're okay otherwise?"

"I think so. I guess I'm lucky," George murmured with a note of irony in her voice.

Frank skied up in a *whoosh* of spray. "Come on. We'd better get you to a doctor," he said. "Can you stand up?"

With Nancy and Frank supporting her, George struggled to her feet. "I can stand, but I sure can't ski," George said, wincing.

"I'll get the medics," Frank offered. "They can send a stretcher."

"No, no. I can walk back up to the lift," George insisted. "It's just my wrist. But it really does hurt!" Pain was written all over George's face.

"I never saw skis snap like that," Frank muttered under his breath. "Especially new ones . . ."

Nancy read the frown on his face and knew what it meant. "I know," she said. "I don't like it one bit, either."

Nancy and Frank helped George back up to the top of the trail and into a chair lift. Within a few minutes they were sitting in the lodge's infirmary and the resort's doctor was gently examining George's purple wrist—it hadn't swollen too badly.

"We'll put a cast on, and I want you to leave it alone for at least ten days, understand?" Dr. Mansfield said, his black eyes snapping. "No monkey business."

"You mean 'no skiing,' right?" George asked.

"That's exactly what I mean, young lady," the doctor replied. "Not that I expect you'll be tempted. You couldn't even hold a ski pole with that wrist."

"I'll be good, Doctor." George looked pretty upset. Nancy knew how much she'd looked forward to skiing at Mount Mirage.

"This is a big resort"—Dr. Mansfield was trying to comfort George—"and there are lots of things to do. Now, hold still while I put this splint on your arm."

The wall phone rang, and Dr. Mansfield picked it up. "Infirmary," he said. His bushy gray eyebrows drew together as he listened to the person on the other end of the line. "Mmmm—I'll be right there. Yes—just tell her to lie down and not to exert herself."

He hung up and turned to George with a smile. "The splint is in place, but I'm afraid you'll have to wait for the nurse to put the cast on. It seems that there's a guest who's going into labor. Be careful, and come back tomorrow to let me know how you're doing." He packed up his black bag and left the room.

"I think you're incredibly brave, George.

That thing must hurt like crazy," Nancy said, putting a reassuring arm around her friend's shoulder. "Hey! Look who's here!"

Frank Hardy poked his head in the doorway and looked around. "Did you put that splint on yourself, George? Nice work!" he said, laughing.

"Don't be silly. The doctor was called away," George responded.

"Isn't there a nurse?" he asked.

Nancy shrugged. "The doctor said she'd be back in a minute."

"Could you come with me for a minute, Nan? There's something I want to show you. It's important, or I wouldn't drag you away right now." From the urgency in Frank's tone, Nancy knew something was definitely up.

Nancy looked over at her friend. "Will you be all right?"

"Sure, go ahead," George replied. "I can manage. It's a whole lot easier waiting here than being buried alive in a snowbank."

"We'll be right back," Frank assured her.

Frank was silent as they went up in the elevator. Nancy assumed he didn't want to talk in front of other people. Beyond that, his features were unreadable. She wondered what was going on.

Inside his room, Frank locked the door and pointed Nancy toward the bed. "Get a load of that."

Frank had arranged George's skis on the bed. Nancy examined the place where the right ski had snapped in two. "Turn it over," Frank urged her.

As soon as she did, Nancy immediately saw what Frank was getting at. "It's been partially sawed through," she said.

"You'll notice that whoever did it was clever enough to disguise the work." He pointed to the spot. "Nancy, the way this is going, somebody's going to get killed—"

"And it looks as if Ken's the prime target," Nancy finished for him. "These were his skis." Nancy was running her fingers over the break. The saboteur had used a miniature jigsaw, she concluded from the almost imperceptible saw marks. A specialist's tool. The wire that had been used to sabotage the lifts was very special, too. Was there a connection?

Frank interrupted her thoughts. "There is a possibility that someone is out to get George and not Ken."

Nancy looked up, surprised. "You're right. I hadn't thought of that. But that doesn't seem likely, does it?"

"Not as likely as someone getting Ken. But we have to cover all possibilities," Frank said.

Nancy nodded. "You're right. We can't rule out anything. Meanwhile, what's our next move?"

"It could take us forever to check out all the

employees systematically." Frank pulled the list out of his pocket and held it out with a helpless gesture.

"And we're racing against the clock now. It looks like our saboteur is out to kill." Nancy agreed.

"Let's see if we can narrow it down," Frank said. "Any suspects?"

"I keep thinking about that Pete Dawson," Nancy said. "He seemed like he had a pretty hostile attitude. And he's a handyman, which means he's got access to saws and wires and other necessary equipment."

"And he'd have to be a good skier to live in that house on the slope," Frank said. "Who knows what his motive might be, but he fits the bill. But so might a few others on that list," he pointed out.

Nancy bit her lower lip. "Well, we've got to start somewhere. What do you say we tail him for a while and see what happens?"

"Okay by me. Why don't I keep an eye on him? You can find Ken and explain what happened with his skis. He should know about it."

"You're right." Nancy felt a flush come over her as she realized that as they'd been talking, she and Frank had drawn closer and closer together. By now, their faces were just inches apart. His brown eyes were staring deeply into hers. What if . . . ?

Before she could finish her thought, Nancy stepped back nervously. "Well, I guess George is waiting for us," she said, breaking the spell.

Frank coughed. "Right." He leaned over to pick up the skis, and hid them in the back of his closet. "Evidence," he explained, following Nancy to the door. "After you."

They stepped out into the hall just as Dr. Mansfield came by, scratching his head.

"Headed back downstairs, Doctor?" Nancy asked him. "How's the baby?"

The doctor looked at her. "I don't understand it," he muttered. "There was nobody there. I'm sure I got the room right—229. I asked twice. Now, why would somebody play a prank like that?"

Nancy and Frank looked at each other. George was in the infirmary—alone!

"Come on, Doctor!" Nancy shouted, grabbing him by the arm. "We've got to get to the infirmary, quick!"

Frank and Nancy took the stairs, instead of waiting for the elevator. The bewildered doctor was at their heels. They rushed down the hall and burst into the room. Nancy was gasping for breath as she stopped dead in her tracks.

George was lying on the floor—motionless!

Chapter Seven

"I THINK SHE'S coming around," Dr. Mansfield murmured a few seconds later, kneeling at George's side, Nancy and Frank next to him.

"Thank goodness," Nancy whispered. Her friend's dark lashes began to flutter, and then slowly her eyelids flickered and slid back.

"Hello there, George," Frank said, sounding calm and reassuring.

"What happened?" George blearily looked up at Nancy, trying to focus her eyes.

"That's what we want to know," the doctor said.

"Looks like somebody conked you over the head. You'll be all right in a little while." Frank put a hand around George's shoulder and helped raise her to a sitting position.

Nancy watched as Frank and the doctor helped George to sit on the examining table. "This hasn't been your day, has it?" she asked her friend with a sad smile. Nancy gently smoothed the hair back off George's forehead while Dr. Mansfield studied the bump on the back of her skull.

"How did it happen, George?" Frank wanted to know.

George didn't answer; she only looked confused. She glanced around the room as if she were trying to orient herself. "I remember—I was over there, looking out the window, and I heard the door open. I thought it was you, Doctor. But there was only this guy wearing a ski mask. The next thing I knew, I was on the floor. And that's all I remember." George lay back and closed her eyes.

"It's my fault. We shouldn't have left her alone," Frank said, gritting his teeth in frustration.

"Don't be so hard on yourself, Frank," Nancy protested.

Frank shook his head. "The stakes are getting too high for us to make any more mistakes."

"What do you mean?" George asked weakly.

"I'll tell you later," Nancy said, giving her

friend's shoulder a squeeze. "Close your eyes and rest now."

George took her friend's advice. Dr. Mansfield, who had finished examining the bump on George's head, began plastering her wrist.

"Frank, this doesn't make sense. Why would anyone be after George?" Nancy asked. "She hasn't got an enemy in the world. And if they're after us because we're detectives—well, *we're* the detectives, not her!"

Frank nodded. "As far as we can tell, there's no reason for the saboteur to target George," he concluded. "So if she got hit over the head, maybe it was because she was in the wrong place at the wrong time."

"What do you mean?" Nancy asked, struggling to understand.

"Why call the doctor away?" Frank asked. He answered his own question. "So someone could have access to the infirmary."

"Of course!" Nancy cried. "There has to be something here that the saboteur wants!" Turning to Dr. Mansfield, she said, "Doctor quick—where do you keep your supplies?"

The doctor looked startled. "Most of them are in that closet." He went over and opened a large cabinet. "What? Half of my supplies are missing!"

"What do you keep in that closet?" Frank wanted to know.

"Everything—all my supplies and medicine."

"Even poisonous materials?" Frank asked. The doctor nodded.

Frank and Nancy caught each other's eye. "How long would it take you to check your inventory and give us a list of what's missing?" Nancy asked the doctor.

Dr. Mansfield thought for a moment. "A couple of hours," he replied. "Maybe less."

"Please hurry," Nancy told him. "It may be a matter of life and death. Come on, Frank."

Frank was ready. "Where to?" he asked.

"To see Ken Harrison." Nancy stopped in her tracks. "Oh, but I can't leave George."

"I'll keep an eye on her," the doctor promised.

"I'll be fine, Nancy," George said weakly. "Don't let me hold you back, please."

"Well, if you're sure," Nancy said, giving her friend's good hand a squeeze. "We're going to need you later."

Nancy followed Frank out of the infirmary and toward the main lobby.

"Should we try his office first?" Nancy asked.

"Good idea." Frank nodded and steered them both in the direction of the lounge.

"I just hope Joe and Bess are making headway, too," Nancy said as she knocked on Ken Harrison's office door.

Frank grinned at her. "Knowing Joe, he's probably doing just fine."

"Come in," Ken's voice called out from behind the thick oak door.

Nancy turned the knob and pushed the door open. Ken was on the phone but quickly hung up when he saw who it was.

"What can I do for you?" he asked.

Frank explained what had happened to George's skis on the slopes and how someone had broken into the infirmary. When he told Ken their theory that someone may have been looking for poison, Ken looked shocked.

"Ken, think hard," Nancy implored. "Is there someone who'd like to see you dead?"

Ken leaned back in his chair and shook his head nervously.

"Anyone from the past? Anyone you ever fired?" Frank stopped his pacing to ask.

"If anyone pops into your head, say it," Nancy recommended. "We can always discard candidates if they're innocent."

Ken let out a sigh. "If there is someone who wants to kill me, I honestly don't know who it could be," he told them, throwing up his hands.

Nancy let out a sigh of her own. The situation on Mount Mirage was going from bad to worse, and they weren't even close to solving it. And that night half the guests were going to be at the big party in honor of the videotaping of "High Life." What better time to hurt Ken or the resort or both?

"Okay. Let me suggest something to you." Frank flopped down in one of Ken's overstuffed leather chairs. "What about Pete Dawson? How well do you know him?"

Ken looked over at Frank in surprise. "Pete? Why, he's been here his whole life! His dad worked for me when we were first setting up the place."

"Have you ever had any problems with him?" Nancy asked gently.

"Problems with Pete? Well, not—not exactly," Ken said hesitantly. "He's always been—well, strange, but nothing I could put my finger on."

Nancy's and Frank's eyes met. "What do you know about him, Ken?" Nancy asked.

"Let's see. He lives up in his father's old cabin on the slopes," Ken told her. "His dad was a miner before there were any skiers around here, and he worked out of that shack. When I opened the resort, I offered Pete a new apartment down the hill, near the rest of the staff, but he said no. I guess he's attached to the place."

"Are there still mines up there?" Frank asked.

"Not exactly. There was some gold mining a few miles from here back at the beginning of the century. And there's an old legend about gold in the area. But Pete's dad and the other dreamers who staked their claims around here never got rich on the gold from this mountain." He smiled. "That's why it's called Mount Mirage."

"What was Pete's father like?" Nancy asked.

"He was a crazy old coot," Ken answered with a laugh. "Young Pete is still looking for gold, but he's more sophisticated about his search. I hear he has a regular little lab in his house."

Pete Dawson had a lot of interesting talents, Nancy thought. "I'll bet he's a pretty fair skier, too," Frank suggested, as if reading her mind.

"Oh, he's good, all right," Ken answered with a smile. "He'd give anyone a run for his money."

Frank shifted in his chair. "Ken, we're going to be watching Pete, if you don't mind."

Ken sighed heavily and leaned back in his chair. "Do what you have to, but I can't believe Pete's the man. He's not the most emotionally stable person I know, but he's harmless. I can't imagine him wanting to hurt me or the resort. Frankly, what I'm concerned about is tonight. You're going to be there, aren't you?"

"We'll all be there," Frank told him.

"Remember, Archer Lampley doesn't know a thing about the problems we've been having here," Ken emphasized. "If he knew, he'd take the entire 'High Life' cast and crew and fly them out of here, and that would be disastrous for Mount Mirage."

"No problem. He doesn't have to know a thing about us," Nancy answered him.

Before Nancy could continue, the door flew open and Raven Maxwell blew into the room. Without acknowledging Nancy or Frank, she went up to Ken. "Listen, I need to go over this schedule with you right away!"

In less than a minute she had talked him through the entire shooting schedule for the rest of the day and evening. Ski footage was almost done shooting, then the crew would set up to film the toasts for a documentary based on the making of the video. Charity donors mingling with the stars, that sort of thing.

"So you know where we're going to be shooting. Is there anything going on I should know about?" She leaned her clipboard against her hip.

Ken hesitated for a moment and looked away from Nancy and Frank. "No, there's nothing," he said, smiling weakly.

"Good. Well, then, I'll see you later." In another instant she was gone.

"Whew! She's a whirlwind." Frank's eyes were wide. Raven Maxwell certainly made an impression wherever she went.

Nancy wondered to herself why Ken hadn't told Raven the latest incidents. Maybe he was worried the news would get back to Lampley.

"Let's see if there's anyone else we should be keeping an eye on," Frank said, riffling through his employee lists. One of the pages slipped out of his hand and fell under Ken's desk.

Frank bent down to retrieve it, but when he stood up again, he wasn't holding the paper. Instead he was clutching a small metal object. He held it up for Nancy to see.

"Look familiar, Detective Drew?" Frank asked.

Nancy knew what it was at once.

Ken looked at them quizzically.

"It's an electronic bug," Nancy explained. "Someone's been spying on you, Ken!"

Chapter Eight

KEN'S PALE EYES widened in astonishment. "A bug," he mumbled. "Wow!"

"A very sophisticated one, too," Nancy threw in. "I've seen equipment like this before. It's very expensive."

Frank pocketed the bug. "I'll get rid of this later," he said. "Whoever is spying on you will know you're on to him, but we don't have much of a choice."

Ken was shaking his head. "I can't believe this is happening to me. I have such a bad feeling about tonight," he muttered.

"Try not to worry, Ken," Nancy told him. "We're going to get to the bottom of this."

"I hope so," said Ken as Nancy and Frank headed out the door.

"Count on it," Frank told him, with a smile that made Ken's eyes brighten a little. Outside in the lounge, Frank turned to Nancy. "Well, what do you think?"

"I don't know. I'm starting to think it's more complicated than simple sabotage."

Frank asked, "Why?"

Nancy frowned. "That electronic bug shows a degree of sophistication that goes far beyond sabotage."

"I see—" Frank broke off when he saw a familiar figure heading their way. "Jack Treyford at two o'clock," he muttered under his breath.

"Hello!" Treyford called to Nancy. "Didn't I see you on the slopes earlier today?"

"Yes, you did. Hello, Mr. Treyford," Nancy replied.

"You are?" the developer asked.

"Nancy. Nancy Drew. And this is my friend, Frank Hardy."

"Hello," the developer said affably. He looked handsome in his crisp formal wear, with a red plaid cummerbund. On his arm was a beautiful, dark-haired woman who was looking up at him adoringly.

Treyford continued, "Allow me to introduce my fiancée, Inez Ibarra. Inez, Nancy Drew and Frank Hardy."

"Pleased to meet you," Inez Ibarra said in a sultry voice. Then she turned back to Treyford with a puppy-dog look.

"Hi," Nancy murmured. Inez Ibarra, of course! She'd seen that face on the covers of dozens of magazines. Inez Ibarra was one of the world's top models.

"Actually, I was wondering about your friend," Treyford continued. "The dark-haired young lady? I was there when she took that fall. Is she all right?"

"She broke her wrist, but she'll be okay," Nancy answered.

"Thank goodness," said Treyford with a smile. "Well, I'm off to Ken Harrison's office before we have our cocktail hour. Our heated sidewalk is completely frozen, and I want to tell him about it personally."

Hmmm, thought Nancy. Here's a chance to see exactly what Treyford's connection is to Harrison.

She remembered Ken telling them that Treyford owned a condo at Mount Mirage. But that didn't give him the right to constantly criticize Ken.

"What a coincidence!" she said impulsively, taking Frank's arm. "We were just on our way there ourselves."

"Really?" Treyford looked perplexed. "You're headed the wrong way."

"Oh?" Nancy scrambled for an explanation.

"Oh, right! This place is so immense, I just get lost. Right, Frank?"

Frank gave her a strange look. "Right, Nancy," he said with a crooked smile.

Treyford looked dubious, but he didn't press it. The two couples walked back to Ken's office together. Ken was still there, seated behind his desk. When he saw Frank and Nancy, he looked surprised but didn't say anything.

"Hello, Ken," Treyford said, with an edge in his voice. "I thought you might like to know that our heated sidewalk is not functioning properly. Inez almost tripped on the way to the lodge."

Nancy looked down at the model's sleek high heels and suppressed a smile.

"And as long as we're chatting, there is also the matter of the snack bar. Are you aware that paper napkins have been substituted for cloth ones this week?"

Treyford's eyes were full of contempt. "I mention these things because, as you know, I also manage properties. When a property carries the Treyford name, however, every detail is seen to. If I can't afford the best, I'd rather not be in business. That's an attitude you should explore."

Ken let the insult pass. "I'll see about the heated sidewalks," he told the developer calmly, but Nancy heard the anger in his voice.

"This certainly isn't a Treyford property,"

the developer added, making his way to the door.

"It certainly isn't," Ken called after him. "And it never will be! No matter how much you offer me for it!"

"We'll see! See you at the toast tonight!" Treyford said, almost cheerfully. "Come, Inez."

Without a word, the model obediently followed Treyford out the door.

Aha, Nancy thought, exchanging a look with Frank. That explained why Treyford bothered to get so involved with the management of Mount Mirage. It was simply a personal interest.

When they were gone, Nancy looked at Ken. "I didn't know he'd offered to buy this place from you," she said.

"Oh, yes," Ken replied distractedly. "He's been hounding me for nearly two years now. He's really persistent, too. I've had other offers, but his is still far and away the highest. But I'm not Treyford, and I'm not selling, to him or anybody. I love this place."

Nancy couldn't help noticing the calm determination in Ken's voice. Now she understood why he'd asked both Nancy *and* the Hardys to stop the sabotage campaign. To Treyford, Mount Mirage would be a business. To Ken Harrison, it was his life.

* * *

"I just can't believe it! He kissed me!" Bess was wildly excited. She was breathless, and her eyes had about a million stars in them. "Brad MacDougal actually kissed me!"

"Take it easy, Bess." George laughed, lying in bed with her right arm in a sling. "I'm sure Brad MacDougal's kissed lots of girls before. He'll probably kiss a lot more in the future, too."

"I'll never wash this cheek again!" Bess said, ignoring her cousin's practical remark. "Thank you, universe, my life's dream has been fulfilled!"

"Until tomorrow anyway," Nancy teased, with a wink at George.

"So what else happened? Let's hear the juicy details," George put in. "Did you guys talk to each other at all? You said you were together for forty-five whole minutes."

"Sure we talked. I learned all about his life before he became a star. And—oh, I forgot to tell you about the Archer Lampley thing!" Bess said, reminding herself.

Nancy looked up, her interest piqued. "What about Archer Lampley?" she asked.

"Brad had another fight with him!" Bess said. "A really intense one, too. I thought someone was going to get hurt, namely Mr. Lampley. Brad is incredibly strong. You should check out his muscles, they're like steel."

"I'll pass on the muscles. What happened?" George wanted to know.

"Well, Mr. Lampley came by and asked Brad if he was going to apologize for last night, and Brad just exploded! It was really weird. In one second he went from being this sweet, sweet guy to an absolute madman. He grabbed Mr. Lampley by the lapels and shouted into his face that he was going to kill him! Then he let go of him, and after Mr. Lampley left the room, he was sweet, gentle Brad again. It was unbelievable."

Nancy looked at George, then at Bess. "Maybe you ought to give it a rest where Brad's concerned, Bess," she warned. "He seems a little unstable to me."

"Me, too," George agreed.

"You guys," Bess complained, a hurt look on her face. "I thought you trusted my judgment."

There was a knock on the door, and Frank Hardy poked his head in. "We're meeting at seven o'clock, right?" he asked. "In our room?"

"Right," Nancy nodded. "We'll be there."

"Good. Oh, by the way"—Frank looked a little concerned—"has anybody seen Joe?"

Joe was with Roseanne James, sitting across from her in the nearly empty Skytop restaurant. In front of them were half-empty cups of hot chocolate.

"Ken was in love with my mother, you know. She loved him, too, I've been told. I was just a year old when they met, but I heard all about it." The singer's lovely eyes filled with tears.

"After that, Archer Lampley signed her up for a national tour. She had to do two and three concerts a day, all over the country. After three years of that, she couldn't take it," Roseanne said, her voice growing soft. "Archer as good as killed her."

Roseanne's eyes took on an angry glow. "I think he's evil. I heard he used to barge into her dressing room and ridicule her singing. He told her it was a good thing the public were fools."

Joe drank in everything Roseanne was telling him, the whole story that had ended in her mother's tragic suicide.

"But, Roseanne"—Joe leaned across the table with a questioning look—"if you found out all that, what made you sign with Archer Lampley?"

Roseanne's response was a heavy sigh. She bit her lip before answering. "I was young, Joe. I didn't think I had a chance with anyone else. And he was right there, telling me all the great things he was going to do for me. . . ."

Roseanne's voice trailed off and a weak smile passed over her lips. "I guess I was crazy."

Joe reached across the table and took her hand. "Thanks for listening to all this," she told him, brushing away a tear. "Now you know everything."

Joe Hardy stared into her eyes, wishing he could erase every hurt she'd ever had. He felt incredibly tender toward this beautiful girl.

"Well, not everything," Roseanne added with a small smile. "There's just one more thing. But if I tell you, you've got to promise you won't hate me."

"I won't hate you, Roseanne," Joe murmured. "I won't ever hate you, I promise."

"Thank you." She squeezed his hand. "What I told you about death threats—it isn't true."

Joe's breath stuck in his throat. He'd sensed she had been lying to him the night before. Now he knew he had been right.

"I didn't bring that gun here to protect myself." Roseanne was crying now, her voice catching, tears rolling down her cheeks. "I brought it . . . so I could kill Archer Lampley."

She burst into great sobs now, her shoulders heaving. She tried to speak, but she couldn't go on.

"It's okay, it's okay," Joe whispered. But of

course it wasn't okay. It wasn't okay at all, and they both knew it.

"Joe," she finally managed to whisper. "I hate him. I hate him so bad—and I can't take it anymore!" Again her sobs overcame her.

"Roseanne," he said levelly, staring into her eyes. "Give me the gun. I'll take it straight to the hotel safe and lock it up, and that will be the end of it."

"I promised myself I would stop him," Roseanne whispered. "I promised myself I'd destroy him."

Joe looked at Roseanne closely. He just didn't believe she could be a murderer. It wasn't possible.

"Give me the gun, Roseanne," he repeated finally. "It's not a crime to hate somebody, especially a creep like Lampley. But guns and hatred are a bad combination. Don't ruin your life with one bad mistake."

Roseanne wiped a tear from her eye. She seemed to be considering Joe's advice carefully. "All right," she said, sighing deeply. Then she sat still for a long moment. Finally, releasing his hand, she reached for her purse under the chair.

Joe watched as Roseanne searched her purse. A moment later she looked up at him, alarmed.

"Joe!" she cried. "My gun—it's gone!"

Chapter Nine

I THINK I like it, Bess," George said with a laugh as she looked at her cousin's curls. "I mean, it sure is different."

"What do you think, Nancy?" Bess asked, as Nancy walked in from the bathroom, a make-up bag in her hand.

A broad streak of Bess's blond hair was dyed hot pink.

"Well, it's . . . different," a surprised Nancy ventured.

"You both hate it, I can just tell." Bess bit her lip and pouted. "Well, at least it'll wash out after ten shampoos."

"We didn't say we hated it, Bess," Nancy

pointed out. "I just said it's different. It's kind of fun, too."

"Yes, but will *Brad* like it? Or is it too loud? Oh, I hope I didn't make a big mistake," Bess moaned.

Nancy looked over at her pretty friend and shook her head. In her off-the-shoulder hot pink dress, Bess looked fabulous.

"I don't think Brad'll be shocked," Nancy threw in. "He seems to have seen it all, if you ask me."

Suddenly sensitive, Bess glared at Nancy in the mirror and started spritzing herself furiously with cologne. "Well, I didn't ask you about Brad," she huffed. "I just wanted to know what you thought of my hair!"

"Don't worry, Bess. He'll love it, if he notices it, that is," George called out from inside the closet, where she was choosing her outfit for the celebrity toast. "By the way, when's the wedding going to be?"

Bess rolled her eyes in annoyance. "You guys," she complained. "Will you please give me a break?" She fluffed the bold yellow feathers dangling in her ears. "I think it works," she decided, regarding her image in the mirror.

"Need help zipping up, George?" Nancy asked, after she had slipped into a teal silk dress and black patent pumps.

"Actually, I do," George answered, emerging from the closet with her rose woolen dress covering her head and shoulders. Nancy tugged the dress down over George's silky slip and reached for the zipper.

"I think Brad is extremely sweet," Bess asserted. "And I think you're both jealous because I spent so much time with him."

George and Nancy exchanged a startled look. Bess was a wonderful girl, but she could go off the deep end.

"Bess, you don't have to be defensive," Nancy offered as gently as she could.

"I notice *you're* spending a lot of time with Frank Hardy, Nan. And I also notice you haven't mentioned Ned once since we got to Mount Mirage." The words hit Nancy like a brick.

"I'm only spending time with Frank because we're working together, Bess!" Nancy declared.

"Now who's defensive, Nancy? Come on, tell me you're not enjoying it. I can see the way you two look at each other," Bess said.

The way George waited for a response made Nancy feel sure that she silently agreed with her cousin's observations.

"Well, I—I do like Frank—" Nancy sputtered, wishing she were able to stop her face from turning red. "I'm not going to deny that—"

Before she could finish, Bess walked over to

her and threw her arms around Nancy's shoulders. "I'm sorry, Nan. It was awful of me to say that. I know how you feel about Ned—really I do."

Bess's embrace was comforting, but it didn't wipe away her words. If her friends could see something happening between her and Frank, could she trust her own feelings?

"I'm ready, how do I look?" George asked, trying to change the subject. Despite the sling, George looked terrific.

"I'm ready, too," Nancy said, leaning toward the mirror to check her makeup. No matter what problems were bothering her personally, she needed to concentrate on business. Her feelings for Frank could really mess up her concentration. And she wasn't about to let that happen. Not tonight. Not ever.

"I'm in heaven!" Frank beamed when he opened the door of his room. "Hey, Joe. Check out the three lovely ladies who just knocked on our door."

"Cut it out, Frank," Nancy murmured with a sheepish grin as she stepped into the Hardys' room. Still, it was fun to dress up and turn a few heads now and then.

"Hey, Bess! Some hair!" Joe exclaimed when he noticed the pink streak. "It's different, but it definitely makes it."

"You could be on a poster in a music store," Frank agreed. "The whole outfit is great!"

Bess shot a triumphant look at her friends and glanced at her image in the Hardys' mirror again. "Thanks, guys."

"So," Frank continued in a back-to-business voice. "Jack Treyford offered to buy Mount Mirage. Do you think that means anything?" He cast a glance around the room.

"It could be an ordinary business proposition," said George. "Treyford and his firm must buy dozens of businesses every year."

"I suppose so," Nancy agreed. "In any case, it's something to keep in mind."

"I have news," Joe announced.

Nancy turned to him. Outwardly, Joe looked like his fun-loving old self, but something behind his eyes was troubled.

"First of all, Roseanne told me she came here to kill Archer Lampley—" he began.

"I don't believe it!" Bess interrupted. "Roseanne James is going to murder someone?"

"Well, Bess, not quite," Joe said slowly. "She said she *wanted* to. She hates Lampley, and she talked herself into getting a gun to do it. But Roseanne couldn't hurt a fly. I convinced her to put the pistol in the lodge safe. But when she went to give me the gun, it was gone."

"This is getting stranger and stranger." Nancy exhaled deeply.

"It is weird," George offered. "There's the sabotage—the trail markers, the snapped ski, and the things Ken told us about. But then there's all this other stuff: Roseanne threatening Archer; Ken and Treyford; Brad threatening Archer. From what you told me, Nancy, I get the feeling there's not a lot of love lost between those last two."

"Well, Brad MacDougal is not a killer, if that's what you think, George!" Bess put in hotly. "He just has an artistic temperament!"

"Roseanne isn't a killer, either." Joe sounded a lot more in control, but his meaning was the same.

"Well, maybe we'll know more after I tail Pete Dawson tonight," Frank said. His eyes met Nancy's for a moment.

"I guess we should get started," Nancy said as she scooped up her black satin evening bag. "Bess, try to find out as much about Brad as you can. And, George, why don't you stay close to Raven Maxwell, okay? She always seems to be in the center of the action."

"Okay, Nan," George said with a nod. "But I have to tell you, I've about had my fill of action."

There was no need to mention Joe's position at Roseanne's side. Joe had elected himself to that job from the moment he'd laid eyes on the beautiful singer.

"Okay," Frank said. "I think we all know what we have to do. Everybody keeps his or her man—or woman, as the case may be—out of trouble for the evening. Let's go."

The group threaded out of the Hardys' door into the hotel corridor. Joe, Bess, and George fell in step together, with Frank and Nancy behind.

"You look a little upscale to be tailing a maintenance man, Frank," Nancy observed with a grin.

"In case I get back in time for the toast, I want to be ready," Frank explained.

"True." Nancy nodded. "There's Pete now." She had seen him the moment they rounded a corner. He was talking to Ken Harrison.

"If I do, it's for a good cause. But I'm sure glad I decided to wear boots tonight."

Surprised, Nancy looked down at Frank's feet. She hadn't noticed his thick snowboots before. "Good thinking," she commented appreciatively.

Nancy and Frank approached Pete Dawson and Ken, who were standing by the window, deep in conversation. "Good luck, Frank," Nancy whispered.

"Okay, okay. I said I'll do it," Pete was grumbling. Then, with a quick glance in the direction of Frank and Nancy, Dawson stormed away. Frank casually moved off after him.

"Nancy! George! Bess! You look lovely. And hello, Joe." Although he was tense, Ken was trying to appear calm. "How do we stand?" he asked under his breath, waving to guests as they passed on their way into the lounge.

"All four of us are covering the lounge," Joe told him. "Frank's on Dawson tonight."

Ken nodded. "Good, good," he said. "Shall we go in?"

They followed him into the lounge. The spacious room was arranged for the occasion, with round tables grouped toward the center and a dais at one end for the VIPs. Cameras were on raised platforms on either side of the room.

Nancy noticed that most of the tables were already full. Aside from people she assumed must be contributors, she recognized the pop-music personalities who had volunteered for the backup chorus of "Living the High Life For Love," as well as executives of World Children's Charities—about a hundred people in all, Nancy estimated.

Ken Harrison was just sitting down at the center of the dais. Archer Lampley was on his right. Lampley and Ken smiled at each other and began to chat. Raven Maxwell was whizzing around the room, tossing out instructions as she went.

On the other side of Ken sat Brad MacDougal, surveying the scene with an amused smile. When the teenagers walked in, Brad stood up and blew Bess a kiss.

"You see? He really likes me!" Bess whispered to George. She blew him a kiss back.

Jack Treyford was sitting next to Brad, with Inez Ibarra on his left. Treyford was waving to acquaintances in the crowd and seemed to be genuinely enjoying himself. Inez had a plastered-on smile in place, as though she were there to be looked at. *It comes from being a model*, Nancy thought.

To the right of Archer Lampley sat Roseanne James, looking white as a sheet. Archer whispered in her ear occasionally, which made her cringe.

Joe and the others found their table and seated themselves. Every time Lampley leaned close to Roseanne or gave her hand a squeeze, Joe started to steam. Fortunately, he was keeping a lid on his emotions.

But as far as Nancy was concerned, there was no doubt about it—Joe Hardy had it bad for Roseanne James.

A portly middle-aged man was seated next to Roseanne. He held some three-by-five index cards in one hand, and he was studying them.

On his right, looking thrilled to be there, was Chester L. Peabody, the inventor–lottery millionaire. His wife, seated next to him, seemed equally pleased.

"What did Chester Peabody do to get himself seated up there?" Nancy asked out loud.

"He's donating a million dollars to the cause." Raven Maxwell's voice made Nancy jump a little. The woman always seemed to be there with the answers.

"Wow! A million dollars!" Bess's mouth had dropped open. "Is he the biggest contributor?"

"Not by half," Raven said, rolling her eyes. "Treyford's donating two million. He's always got to be the biggest and best at everything."

The portly man stood up and faced the crowd. "Ladies and gentlemen," he began as the cameras rolled on either side of him. "I'm Harold Morston of World Children's Charities. Tonight our organization will celebrate its finest hour. All of what we're doing here this week—the great music, the videotaping, the skiing, the sports exhibitions, the celebrations—it's all for one purpose. To help kids!" Here he was interrupted by a heartfelt round of applause.

"Most of you have already signed over your checks," he went on. "But two of our biggest contributors are about to fork it over right here and now, as it were—" Laughter interrupted him. "Let's begin with Mr. Chester L. Peabody."

The crowd applauded. Chester got up and raised his glass. "The greatest gift is to be able to give," he said. "I am a very lucky man, and I'm glad that Worldwide Children's Charities exists, so I can spread some of that luck around." Chester signed his check to enthusiastic applause.

Jack Treyford was next. Thanking Chester, he promptly upped his contribution to an astonishing three million! The crowd gasped, then gave him a standing ovation.

Beaming, Harold Morston spoke again. "Thank you! Thank you both, and thank you all! Now, I'd like to turn the mike over to Mr. Archer Lampley, the producer of the music and the video that will benefit so many children in so many ways."

Archer Lampley rose to his feet and met the applause of the assembly with a modest bow. Nancy noticed that everyone, even Ken and Roseanne, seemed more relaxed as they got caught up in the event around them.

"Thank you so much," Lampley told the crowd. "But I'm afraid an even bigger hand should go to two of America's brightest stars—Mr. Brad MacDougal and the lovely and talented Ms. Roseanne James."

The applause grew as Roseanne and Brad

got up and waved to the crowd. Bess and Joe both stood up, applauding. George and Nancy, looking at each other and smiling, got up, too. Soon the whole room was standing again.

Roseanne and Brad walked into a spotlight, the room lights dimmed, and as music came from hidden speakers, they began singing:

"I've been around the world,
I've seen it all,
I've tasted fine champagne
I've partied in Nepal,
But it's not fame and fortune
That I'm fondest of, no,
I'm livin' the high life for love . . ."

When the song was finished, the excited crowd rose to its feet and cheered. Archer Lampley calmed them down, then took his glass and raised it. "Ladies and gentlemen, I drink this toast to you! To all of you who have made this possible." He downed his glass of champagne, and the guests downed theirs.

Everyone waited for Lampley to say something more, but he just stood there, with a surprised look on his face. The look soon became a grimace, then his face turned red and then an unnatural shade of blue.

Archer Lampley dropped his champagne glass to the floor, where it shattered into a thousand pieces. Then, with a horrible choking sound, he slumped to the floor!

Chapter Ten

As Lampley's body hit the floor, a shocked murmur ran through the room. Joe Hardy leapt up, shoved his way over to the collapsed promoter and manager, and waved everyone off. "Make room! Give him air!" he shouted.

Lampley was gasping for breath and was in obvious pain. His eyes seemed to be searching for something, struggling to see clearly. They focused and, for one incredible moment, opened wide. With a groan, Lampley lifted his hand and pointed his finger at Roseanne James. Then he fell back to the floor.

"It can't be!" Roseanne sounded on the edge of total hysteria. "No!" she cried.

Joe put his fingers on Lampley's neck, feeling for a pulse. From the look in Joe's eyes, he didn't find one. Nancy watched as Joe shook his head sadly.

From her place near the stage, Roseanne James watched in horror, then let out a terrified scream. The crowd erupted into a frenzy. Suddenly all the tables were buzzing with animated conversation, and everyone was trying to get a better view of the dais.

Horrified, Nancy looked at the people around her. She saw Raven Maxwell standing off from the crowd, next to a cameraman. The woman looked absolutely stunned.

Brad MacDougal stood over Archer's lifeless body, looking lost, confused, and frightened.

Joe finally stood up. "I'm not getting any pulse," he said quietly.

Jack Treyford stepped away from the dais with his arm around Inez. Nancy thought he had a strange, almost disappointed look on his face.

Ken Harrison, on the other hand, was clearly devastated. People were crowded around him, asking questions, to which Ken could give only the most perfunctory answers. Poor Ken, Nancy thought. He'd seen this coming—or something like it—and he'd been powerless to stop it.

"Did somebody call a doctor?" a voice said at the door, and Dr. Mansfield came bustling in. Nancy went over and led him to where Lampley had fallen. "Tell me what happened," the doctor said.

"He had just drunk a champagne toast," Nancy told him. "Then he went into a kind of spasm, and his face turned blue. After about ten seconds, he fell. Joe checked his pulse, but—"

"Thank you," said Dr. Mansfield, bending down to attend to Lampley's body. "Sounds like a heart attack to me."

"A heart attack?" Nancy asked. "Are you sure?" Her instincts told her that things were too strange at Mount Mirage for Lampley's death to be from natural causes.

Before the doctor could answer, Chester L. Peabody tapped him on the shoulder. The little man looked intensely worried.

"I'm afraid that was no heart attack," Peabody said softly.

Dr. Mansfield stood up. "Who are you?" he asked, frowning.

"The name's Peabody. I know a bit about chemicals, and I have to tell you that when Mr. Lampley collapsed, there was the smell of almonds in the air."

Almonds! Nancy gasped. She knew that the deadly poison cyanide gave off that distinctive odor. Lampley must have been poisoned!

"Are you saying this man was murdered?" Dr. Mansfield demanded.

At the mention of the word *murder,* a buzz passed through the room again. Ken Harrison, whose face had gone white momentarily, quickly recovered his composure and took control of the situation.

"Ladies and gentlemen, please remain calm," he said, holding up his hands for silence. "We'll call the police, and I'm sure they'll be able to sort things out. Until then, if you would all be so kind as to stay at your tables. Please, let me emphasize, there is no danger to any of you."

As the guests began returning to their tables, Nancy walked over to Bess, who was standing with Brad MacDougal. Brad looked pale and shaken. "Poor Archer," he murmured. "I just can't believe it."

Ironic, thought Nancy as she left Bess to comfort Brad. Death had managed to cure all Brad's negative feelings for his manager. Or was Brad just putting on an act?

Crossing the room, Nancy heard Chester Peabody speaking with his wife. "Cyanide's everywhere, Pearl!" he was insisting. "You can't go and outlaw cyanide just because some people use it for murder!"

"Mr. Peabody," said Nancy, moving over to his table. "What do you mean, cyanide is everywhere?"

"Ah, Nancy Drew. Well, let's see." The

inventor stared back at Nancy and pursed his lips. "It's mostly used in metallurgy, for testing precious metals and such. By itself, cyanide is a perfectly harmless substance."

"Isn't this terrible?" Pearl Peabody gave Nancy a look of utter horror. "That poor man gets up to make a speech, and all of a sudden—" Pearl shook her head.

Nancy nodded sadly. "I know," she murmured.

Nancy spotted Frank Hardy at the door. The police were arriving, too.

"Excuse me," she told the Peabodys before she crossed to meet Frank.

"I heard what happened," said Frank. "But guess what? Pete Dawson was nowhere near this place all night. He was at his cabin until about twenty minutes ago. Then he got a phone call. I guess it was about what happened here. He skied down to the lodge, and I followed him."

Nancy frowned. "Frank, this may sound crazy, but what if there were two crimes going on here?"

Frank blew out his breath. "Happens sometimes," he replied.

"Attention, everybody!" A police officer was on the dais now. "I want you to know, we appreciate your patience. We will be coming around to ask each of you what you saw earlier this evening, but we can't get to all of you at once. Please, be patient. Thank you."

A general murmur went through the room. The crowd suddenly seemed anxious to leave the banquet room.

"Frank, you're back." Behind them, Nancy heard George's voice. It had a grim ring to it. "This is all so horrible."

Nancy put a comforting arm around George's shoulders. "Come on," she suggested. "We might as well get back to our table."

On the way Nancy noticed Joe talking to Roseanne. The singer had her face in her hands, and she was sobbing.

"Whew, this is something," Frank murmured as he settled into his seat. "What happened? Tell me everything."

Nancy was about to launch into the story when Raven Maxwell approached the table. "Listen," she said in a brusque voice, "I need to know two things from you guys. How long will it take the police to clear the people out of here? And do you think we'll be able to shoot tomorrow?"

Nancy could hardly believe her ears. Was Raven actually planning to go ahead and shoot the rest of the video on schedule?

"I'm not sure," Nancy answered.

"Well, I can't let what happened blow our

whole schedule. Archer would have wanted to go on, too, you know," Raven explained lamely. She must have realized how callous she was sounding.

"Does it really matter anymore?" Frank asked her.

"It certainly does!" Raven snapped. "I'm a professional. If Archer's gone, that means 'Living the High Life for Love' becomes *my* project."

With those words, Nancy realized Raven Maxwell had a solid motive for Archer Lampley's death.

"Raven," Nancy asked, "do you have any tape from tonight? You were filming it, weren't you?"

"Sure, I have tape of the whole incident," Raven told them. "If you want to look at it, we can go into the control room."

Nancy, Frank, and George stood up and followed the producer into the makeshift control booth that had been set up at the far end of the dining room. Raven picked up a tape and inserted it into a monitor.

"There we go." Nancy watched as Roseanne James began to sing. The camera was focused on her in close-up, and it was impossible to see what was happening at the dais. "This is when the cyanide had to be poured into the drink, right, Frank?"

"You're right, Nancy. But this video's no help," Frank said. "It doesn't show the head table or the podium."

"Try this," said Raven, ejecting the tape they were watching and inserting another.

"Shots of the dais!" Nancy said.

Frank's eyes sparkled with excitement. "There's the waiter. Could we slow that up?"

Raven set the machine to play frame by frame. The waiter performed his function perfectly, without a hint of anything suspicious. "It looks like he's innocent," Nancy said.

"Now here's where Archer picks up his glass," said Frank. "Wait a minute!"

Just then the video screen was filled with muted gray and white horizontal stripes. Ejecting the tape, Nancy gave it a close look.

"It looks like somebody's been here before us, Frank. The tape's been tampered with. And the murder's been wiped out!"

Music?

Chapter Eleven

FRANK STARED AT the video monitor in shocked disbelief. "How could anybody have erased the tape so quickly?" he asked.

Raven Maxwell had an answer ready. "It's easy. It would take only a minute."

"Man, oh, man," Frank muttered, shaking his head. "Not only do we have a murder on our hands, but a crucial piece of evidence has been destroyed. Whoever did this is playing for keeps, guys."

"What do you think our next step should be?" George asked.

Frank looked at Nancy and was about to

answer when someone pulled back the curtain surrounding the makeshift room. "Nancy Drew? Frank Hardy?" a young police officer asked.

Frank and Nancy nodded.

"Could you come over here, please? The chief would like to meet you."

Frank, Nancy, and George followed the policeman to a large table the staff had set up in a corner. Ken sat with another officer in a khaki uniform. On his shirt was a starred badge bearing the word *Sheriff.*

"I'm Sheriff Brady," he told them. He was a brawny man of about fifty, Frank guessed. His face was weathered, and his eyes were a steely blue. "Wait a minute," he said, turning abruptly to Ken. "Didn't you say there was another one?"

"Joe." Frank and Nancy spoke at the same time.

"He's over talking to Roseanne James. I can get him for you if you want," Frank offered.

"Nah," the sheriff answered with a dismissive gesture. "Won't be necessary. What I've got to say won't take long."

The sheriff cleared his throat. "Now, listen. Mr. Harrison here tells me you're detectives," the sheriff began with a dubious look.

Frank opened his mouth and was about to answer. The sheriff stopped him.

"We're here now," he said, "and your services won't be necessary. You kids just hang around here till we get to you, and when we're done, you run along and have a good time here at Mount Mirage, like kids are supposed to, you hear?"

"Wait a minute," Ken said. "Maybe I wasn't clear. I brought them in because we were having some episodes of sabotage around here, and they've been—"

"Save your breath," the sheriff interrupted gruffly. "First off, this isn't sabotage we're dealing with, it's murder. Second, I don't need a bunch of kids telling me how to conduct my investigation. You got that, everybody?"

Nancy, Frank, and George nodded politely. Inside, though, Frank found himself resenting the sheriff's manner.

"Thank you, kids," the sheriff said, standing up. "That's all for now. Ken, go get yourself some rest."

With a helpless sigh, Ken turned to them. "Sorry about that," he murmured. "They really don't want any civilian help."

"It's just as well," Frank said. "We need to confer among ourselves, anyway. Nancy, I think we should round up Bess and Joe."

They looked over to where Joe was standing with Roseanne. The singer had Joe's jacket over her shoulders, but she was shivering anyway. "Maybe we should leave them alone for a while," Frank said.

"Are you ready for an all-nighter?" Nancy said, looking up at him with a weary grin.

"I guess I have to be," Frank answered with a shrug. "Because I get the feeling we're going to be here for a while."

"You're probably right," Nancy agreed. "Look, George and I will find Bess. She's got to be with Brad somewhere. Why don't you see if you can get Joe to leave Roseanne for a minute or two."

"It's not going to be easy," Frank told her. "But we really need to plan our next move." With that, Frank headed off to where his brother was still comforting Roseanne. As he got closer, Frank overheard Roseanne's voice.

"I feel so guilty!" she was saying as she hid her face in Joe Hardy's shoulder. The two were standing behind the dais.

"Roseanne, that's crazy," Joe said, trying to soothe her.

Frank edged closer. He felt strange about eavesdropping, but Roseanne didn't seem to mind who heard her. And his brother's attention couldn't be drawn away from the girl.

"But I was sitting right next to him, Joe!" Roseanne insisted through her tears. "I came here to kill him, and now he's dead!" A huge sob erupted from her slender body, and she bent her head. "Oh, Joe. They're going to think I did it. I can just tell."

"Come on, now. You're innocent, and

they'll know it right away," Frank heard Joe say.

Roseanne raised herself up and turned to him, gazing deeply into his eyes. "You're sweet, you know it?" she whispered, with a sad smile. "How do you know I didn't do it? Maybe I did! I've been so crazy lately—crazy with hate and bad feelings. When they find out some of the things I said to Archer, they'll think I did it for sure!"

"They'd be wrong. And I'd make them see it." Frank couldn't believe what Joe was saying. He was ruling out one of their prime suspects.

"How?" Roseanne asked.

"Easy," Joe told her. "You may have wanted Lampley dead. But you're much too emotional to commit a crime like this."

"What do you mean? I could have done it—I was *going* to do it!" Roseanne's voice was a desperate whisper.

"You never would have, Roseanne," Joe said, shaking his head. "Oh, maybe if he started in on you, made you furious at any given moment."

"See?" she said.

"But you could never have planned it in advance, timed it so perfectly, and carried it out so coldly. Not you. Besides, you were on stage singing."

"That's true," Roseanne said, surprised.

"Well, thank goodness somebody believes in me. I'm awfully glad I met you, Joe Hardy."

As Frank watched, Joe gazed tenderly at her tearstained face. Then he kissed her softly.

"Oh, Joe," Roseanne murmured softly.

Finally Frank let out a loud cough. Joe turned around to see his brother standing there.

He quickly unwrapped his arms from around Roseanne's shoulders. A deep blush spread over his face. "Frank! Uh—I was just comforting Roseanne. It's not what you think. . . ." he added lamely.

Frank shook his head. "Probably not," he said ironically. "Anyway, Nancy and I need you. We've got to plan some strategy."

"Sure thing." Joe put his hand on Roseanne's arm. "Don't worry," he said tenderly. "Everything's going to be okay."

"Take care of yourself, Roseanne." Frank beckoned with a flip of his head, and Joe followed his brother. There was an embarrassed silence as they made their way over to where Nancy was sitting.

"Where are Bess and George?" Joe asked as he sat down.

"The police are questioning them now. Most of the other guests have been allowed to leave," Nancy told him.

Frank noticed that the crowd in the room was thinning out. He frowned.

"What's wrong, Frank?" Nancy asked.

Frank leaned over and told her about how Joe had been comforting Roseanne James. A shocked look passed over Nancy's face.

"This is getting awfully complicated, Frank," she said.

Frank nodded. He looked up and saw Dr. Mansfield making his way over to them, his black medical bag in hand.

"They've finally finished with me," the doctor said, pointing to one of the police tables. "I gave them the list of the missing chemicals I was drawing up for you."

"What about us?" Nancy asked. "We need that information, too."

The doctor's answer was a sly grin. "I made a copy."

Frank's eyes went to the page the doctor had taken from his pocket and was unfolding on the table.

"Wow," he said, checking over the long list. "Whoever stole all this must have had pretty deep pockets."

Nancy took an edge of the paper and leaned closer to read it. "Morphine. Veronal. Chloroform. Ether. Nitroglycerine. But no cyanide," she concluded.

"Well, I'll leave this with you now and say good night," Dr. Mansfield said.

"Good night, Doctor," Nancy said.

"And thanks," Frank added.

The doctor turned to go and stepped straight into the path of George and Bess. "How's it going, young lady? Is the cast too heavy?" he asked her.

"Not really. But I'll be glad to get out of it," George answered with a weary smile.

With a wave to them all, the doctor walked out of the room.

Nancy motioned for them to sit down. "Frank and I saw the videotapes of tonight's event, but someone erased any evidence of the murder. The police aren't going to help, either."

"Looks like we've got a lot of work to do—on our own," said Frank. "Bess, stay with Brad MacDougal, okay? You seem to be doing well with him."

Bess smiled and blushed to the roots of her pink-streaked hair. "Okay, Frank."

"Frank, I was thinking," Nancy said. "Raven had a motive for getting rid of Archer Lampley, too. Now that he's gone, she's become the producer of 'High Life' and any other project he had in the works."

"Raven does seem awfully ambitious," George put in.

"I have an idea," Frank said thoughtfully. "How would it be if George did some acting? You could tell Raven you're interested in a production career and ask if you can follow her around. You won't have to ask many questions. She seems to be pretty free with information, and she has a lot of it."

"Fine with me," George said, always game for anything.

"Joe seems to be sticking with Roseanne, which is good," Frank went on. "But, Joe," he added. "I have to warn you about getting too involved. She *is* a suspect, after all."

Joe opened his mouth, ready to defend himself. Then he obviously thought better of it.

"That still leaves Pete Dawson, Junior," Nancy reminded him.

Frank frowned. "We'll have to drop our tail on him. I hate to do that, but I think we all agree that solving the murder comes first, and Pete was nowhere near the scene of the crime."

"Right. Now, the poison had to be dropped into the champagne after the last toast was poured, right?" Nancy asked.

"Right," Joe answered with a nod. "Although it could have been dropped in just before."

Nancy bit her lip before she answered. "I doubt it, Joe. It would have been too risky. The ideal time was when the lights went down and everyone's eyes were on Roseanne and Brad. Of course, I suppose Roseanne could have done it when she walked past Archer on her way to the mike."

An uncomfortable silence passed over the

group. None of them wanted Roseanne to be the guilty person.

"What about the waiter who poured the toast?" Bess asked.

"We saw that on video, Bess," Nancy told her. "He's in the clear."

Frank frowned. "Let's go over this again. So far we have Brad MacDougal. He definitely had motive and, possibly, opportunity."

"Frank." Bess reddened. "I promise you Brad had nothing to do with it. I've gotten to know him very well in the last—"

"Two days?" Nancy finished for her.

"Even if you're right, Bess," Frank said, "and I happen to think you are, the police are still going to be looking closely at Brad. He did threaten to kill the guy just a day ago."

Bess looked sad. "I know," she agreed.

"Roseanne's a likely candidate, too, if you ask me," George put in. "She admits she brought a gun here to kill Lampley. And did you see the way she ran out of the room?"

"We're forgetting some others," Joe reminded them. "There's Jack Treyford—"

"He's a snake, I just feel it in my bones!" George erupted. Then she added, "Sorry. I know this isn't a time to be hot-headed."

"That's okay, George," Frank told her. "Instincts are important, too. I've got to admit, Treyford hasn't exactly struck me as being Mr. Nice Guy."

"But he never met Archer Lampley before this week," Nancy reminded them all. "He and Lampley traveled in two completely different circles and didn't have anything to do with each other."

"True." Frank sighed. "Well, the only other person up there was Ken."

"Ken? You think Ken killed Lampley?" Bess asked, a horrified expression on her face.

"He was sitting right next to him," Frank pointed out quietly. "Remember, Ken told us he was once in love with Jocelyn James. If Ken feels the same way Roseanne does, that Archer Lampley destroyed Jocelyn, he has a motive—revenge."

Nancy let out a whistle. "It's tough for me to believe that Ken would commit a murder," she murmured. "Besides, why would he want us around if he was planning one? It doesn't make sense."

"I think Raven is the most likely person to have killed Archer," Bess threw in.

"She *is* cold and calculating," George said thoughtfully.

"And she was buzzing all over the room the whole time. Everybody could see Brad clearly up there on the dais, but Raven was everywhere!" Bess said, excited. "Nobody would have noticed her dropping cyanide into her boss's drink!"

"But I thought she admired Lampley,"

George said. "She spoke about him in glowing terms, didn't she?"

"Speaking of Raven, she's walking over to our table. We'd better keep our voices down," Joe said quietly.

"Hello, everyone." Raven waved as she whipped by them. "Have you all spoken with the police?"

"Yes, we have," Frank answered for them. "How about you?"

"I'm going right now. I guess they're saving the best for last," Raven told them with a tired grin.

"Listen," Nancy said when the producer was out of earshot. "I'd like to check something out, while Raven's over there with the police." Frank saw her glance at her watch. "I guess I've got a while, don't I? Raven will have a lot to talk about."

"Where are you going, Nancy?" Frank asked.

"Raven's room," Nancy answered. "George, you stay with her if she finishes before I get back. Frank, if you need me, you know where I'll be." Flashing her gold passkey at them, she scooted for the door.

Believing Raven had a motive was one thing. Proving it was another. Nancy stopped at the desk to get Raven's room number, then took the elevator up to the third floor. She paused in front of the producer's room, checking to make sure the hallway was clear. Then she used her passkey to open the door.

Inside, she felt for the light and switched it on. Raven's bags lay open on the bed and sofa. Most of them seemed to hold equipment and papers. Nancy went to the bags. She figured that was the place to look for the *real* Raven Maxwell.

A brief search told Nancy there were only clothes in the first suitcase. She carefully replaced everything in its original position.

The second suitcase seemed to hold mostly papers, books, and other reading material. There was also some correspondence and pamphlets, but the contents were so technical that Nancy couldn't decipher them.

Then, under a pile of papers, she noticed a letter from RCI Productions in London, addressed to Raven Maxwell, Lampley Enterprises—FYEO. For Your Eyes Only.

The letter had been opened and read, but Raven obviously thought it was important enough to keep. Nancy unfolded the single sheet of paper and began to read.

Dear Ms. Maxwell:

It was a pleasure speaking with you the other day. As I mentioned, in the event that there are executive changes at your company, RCI would be most interested in negotiating with you. As you know, this would represent a change from our present policy of not cooperating with the current head of Lampley Enterprises.

In other words, Nancy thought, RCI wouldn't work with Archer Lampley. But if he was out of the picture, they'd be willing to consider a multimillion-dollar deal with his replacement. And if that replacement was Raven Maxwell . . . ?

So Raven had a very good reason to want Lampley out of the way. Maybe even a reason worth killing for.

Chapter Twelve

NANCY CAREFULLY REPLACED the letter and hurried out of the room. Although she would have loved to find out even more about Raven Maxwell, there was no telling when the woman might return. That one letter alone had Nancy's mind teeming with new ideas about the case.

As Nancy stepped out of the elevator in the lobby, she saw Bess and Brad coming toward her. Brad was obviously fuming about something, and Bess was doing her best to calm him down.

"Brad, they're just trying to do their job," Bess was saying in a pleading voice.

"Do their job? They don't even know what their job is! They're just small-time, small-town bullies!"

"Brad, please! Take it easy! They'll find out you're innocent. Just give them time!" Bess said.

"Well, hello," Nancy announced, catching her friend's attention.

"Nancy!" Bess said, startled to see her. "Brad's a little ticked off," she quickly explained. "He doesn't think much of the way the police are doing their investigation."

"You said it, I didn't," Brad growled. "Can you believe they actually think *I* killed Archer Lampley? What a crazy idea!"

"Brad, if you're innocent, the police will figure it out sooner or later." Nancy gave the rock star a comforting look.

"Nancy's just teasing," Bess told Brad quickly. "She knows you're innocent."

"If you ask me," Brad huffed, "they ought to leave the whole investigation to you and the Hardys. That would make a lot more sense." He put his arm around Bess's shoulder. "Let's go. I'm sure Nancy has better things to do than listen to me rant."

"Where are you two off to?" Nancy asked.

"We're going to relax in front of the fire for a little while," said Bess, trying to sound casual. "Unless you need my help," she added.

"That's okay. Have a good time," Nancy said with a wink. Her friend blushed. "I want to check in with Frank and Joe. There's not much more you two can do tonight."

"Thanks, Nancy." Brad took Bess's hand and they started down the corridor.

When Nancy arrived at the lounge, Frank was alone at the table, his legs crossed and propped up on the seat next to him. He looked thoughtful.

"Hi," she said, sitting down next to him. "Anything happen while I was gone?"

Frank thought for a moment. "Well, the police interviewed Mr. Treyford and Inez Ibarra, and Chester Peabody and his wife. Then Ken was called back in. He's still with them."

Nancy took a look over her shoulder at the sheriff's table at the far end of the room. Ken seemed to be pleading with the sheriff about something. Then he stood up and walked toward Frank and Nancy, shaking his head in disbelief.

"Can you believe it?" Ken said when he got to their table. "They think *I* did it! Brady wouldn't listen to anything I said about the sabotage, or the work you're doing. He just started grilling me about Archer Lampley and asking me to 'come clean' with him."

Ken slumped into his chair. "I don't know

what to do anymore. Maybe I ought to just sell this place while I can still get something for it." He let out a deep breath and nervously ran his hands through his thick hair.

Nancy was going to give Ken some kind words of reassurance when a police officer called out, "Roseanne James? Is Roseanne James here?"

"Here I am." Roseanne and Joe walked out from behind a huge screen in back of the dais. Joe had his arm around her.

"Ms. James, would you mind following me? The sheriff would like to have a few words with you."

"Sure," Roseanne said bravely. She turned to Joe and kissed his cheek before following the policeman.

Nancy and Frank exchanged a look as they watched the beautiful singer follow the police officer and take a seat opposite the sheriff. Nancy noticed that Roseanne's hands were balled up in fists.

"She's no match for that sheriff," Joe said glumly, flopping down in a chair next to them. "He's tough."

"What's she going to tell him, Joe? Do you know?" Frank asked his brother.

Joe sighed. "I told her to come clean about the gun, but Roseanne kept saying she didn't want to tell them anything. She's afraid they'll think she did it."

Across the room, Nancy could hear Sheriff Brady's voice rising in accusation, but she couldn't make out the words.

"No! You're wrong!" Roseanne's voice rang out in denial. "I didn't!"

Nancy and Frank looked over at Joe, who was biting his lip. "Oh, man," Joe muttered. "If that jerk thinks he can push her around—" He jumped out of his chair, nearly toppling it over.

"Calm down, Joe," Frank told him, putting his hand on his brother's arm. "You're not going to help Roseanne if you blow your cool."

Joe sat back down and slowly nodded in agreement. "I guess you're right."

But when the sheriff started yelling again, and Roseanne could be heard whimpering in response, Joe jumped to his feet. "I'm going over there," he said firmly.

"Oh, no, you're not," Frank said, grabbing his brother by the shoulders. "We need you. You're no good to us, or to Roseanne, if you get in the way of what Brady's doing. I know you're upset, but try to calm down. We can't help her right now."

"Frank's right, Joe," Nancy agreed. "Besides, if Roseanne is innocent, everything will work out for her."

Joe looked at Nancy, then over at where the sheriff was questioning Roseanne. He seemed ready to walk over and rescue the girl but then somehow summoned the resolve to stay put.

"Sorry, guys," he said quietly. "I guess I'm sort of losing my mind on this one."

Frank placed a supportive hand on his brother's shoulder. "Or your heart, maybe," he said softly.

"It's okay, Joe," Nancy told him. "It's late, and we're all a little tense."

Joe nodded. "You're right. I should try to relax a little and not let it get to me."

"Sheriff!" One of the police officers burst through the door followed by three more men in uniform.

"Sheriff!" he called again. Nancy saw he was holding something up in a white cloth. She nudged Frank.

"What have you got there?" Frank asked as he passed by their table.

"Found the cyanide vial, I think," the policeman said excitedly. "We'll have to check it out, but it sure smells like it."

"Where did you find it?" Sheriff Brady asked, running over to meet the policemen.

"It's the craziest thing," the officer said, shaking his head in wonder. "I never would have believed it. She's got such a pure soul in her music, too."

Nancy, Frank, and Joe were on their feet, following the officers back to the table where the sheriff had been questioning the guests.

"I asked you where you found it," the sheriff repeated impatiently.

The policeman held up the vial for them all to see. With his other hand, he pointed to the frightened country singer.

"Right under Roseanne James's pillow!"

Chapter Thirteen

"No!" Roseanne's scream pierced the room. "It can't be! I didn't kill him, I tell you!"

Joe forced himself not to run up to the sheriff's table and pull her away. That would have been stupid. Yet every muscle in his body was poised for action.

"She's hysterical," Sheriff Brady said in disgust. He growled to one of his assistants, "What time is it?"

"Past three A.M.," the assistant answered.

"Too late to go on," Sheriff Brady decided. "We won't put her under arrest—yet. Get the doctor to give her a sedative, and we'll come back tomorrow."

Standing up and gathering his papers, Sheriff Brady shook a finger in Roseanne's face. "Until then, you stay put, young lady," he admonished. "Seal the road," he ordered. "Make sure no one goes anywhere."

He strode across the room, followed by his entourage. Joe caught up with him by the door.

"I'm telling you, Sheriff, you're making a big mistake," he pleaded.

"Calm down, son," Sheriff Brady ordered, pushing through the large double door and into the lobby.

Joe went after him.

"You don't understand," he insisted. "Roseanne couldn't be mixed up in any of this. Anyone in his right mind could tell she's innocent!"

Sheriff Brady walked out of the lodge and headed for a light gray cruiser with the county emblem on the door. "Look, son, nobody's under arrest—yet. When we come back, we'll be keeping an eye on everybody, not just your girlfriend."

"She's not my girlfriend," Joe corrected. "She—" But before he could continue, he felt his brother's restraining hand on his shoulder.

"Calm down, Joe," Frank said.

Behind Frank stood Nancy, looking concerned. "Frank's right, Joe," she said.

"You're pretty headstrong, kid," Sheriff Brady said with a smug smile. "I'd get ahold of that temper if I were you."

Before Joe could reply, Sheriff Brady hopped in his car, slammed the door, and tore off down the mountain, his siren wailing.

"That show-off." Joe gritted his teeth. "I can't stand the way he's treating Roseanne."

"Come on, Joe," Frank counseled. "Give it a rest for tonight. It's late."

Joe nodded. "All right." He turned around and made his way back to the lodge. For the first time he felt the cool air. He'd walked outside without a jacket.

"Let's meet in the morning," Nancy suggested. "We can talk over breakfast. Say, seven?"

"Make it six," Joe said. "Roseanne'll probably wake up by eight, and those idiots will be back here with a warrant for her arrest by nine or ten. I want some time to work on this. Maybe there's a chance we can nail down the real killer."

Nervously running a hand through his blond hair, he looked at Nancy helplessly.

"We'll save her, Joe," she said. "Don't worry—even if they take her in, we can get her released later."

"Sure," Joe said bitterly, kicking a snowdrift. He knew as well as she did that the cyanide vial was an important piece of evidence. And he also knew another damning truth: that Roseanne James had come to Mount Mirage with the express purpose of killing Archer Lampley.

Joe followed Frank and Nancy back inside. "Well, I'm turning in," Nancy said with a yawn. "It's been a long day."

"I'll walk you to your room, Nancy," Frank offered.

"No, that's okay. It's pretty late," Nancy said. "You don't have to."

"I know I don't have to," said Frank quickly, "I want to." Even in his misery, Joe was struck by the eagerness in his brother's voice. Watching them head off together, he couldn't help wondering if both he and his brother were playing with fire.

When Nancy's alarm pierced her dreams at five forty-five, she looked out the window and gave a little gasp.

"George! Bess! Wake up! Look outside!" she cried.

Last night's light snow had turned into a raging blizzard. Nancy couldn't even see the mountain range that had looked so close in clear skies.

"Looks like Joe's prayers have been answered," Nancy murmured to herself and anybody else who was awake enough to listen.

"There's no way Sheriff Brady will be able to get up here to serve a warrant. This is fantastic!"

"What time is it?" a sleepy Bess inquired.

"Ten of six," Nancy replied.

"Ugh. I'm going back to sleep." With that, Bess buried her face in her pillow and turned to the wall.

Nancy felt newly encouraged, full of energy and optimism. She quickly pulled on a pink sweater with padded shoulders and a pair of blue jeans. Then she went over and shook George and Bess awake.

"What's going on?" Bess groaned sleepily.

"Wake up, sleeping beauty," Nancy told her. "You, too, other sleeping beauty. There's a blizzard outside, and we've got a lot of work to do."

"Leave me alone, Nan," Bess managed to say. "I'll get up later."

"Okay, I'm setting the alarm for ten minutes from now. George, make sure Bess gets to the coffee shop, okay? George?"

"I'm awake," George answered groggily. "At least I think I am. Got any aspirin? My wrist is killing me."

Nancy rummaged through the bathroom cabinet and came back into the bedroom to give George a couple of tablets. "Here, George, there's water by your bed. Meet you in the restaurant in a few minutes."

Patting her friend on the shoulder, she flew out the door and down to the restaurant. Frank and Joe were waiting when she walked in.

Joe gave her a big smile. "What do you think of the weather!" he asked, gesturing toward the floor-to-ceiling windows and the raging storm outside. "Thank you, universe!"

"How did you sleep, Nancy?" Frank asked.

"Great," Nancy answered, touched by his concern. "Somehow, getting up was easy, too. This snow has given me a real boost."

"And we're going to solve this thing today, right?" Joe smiled.

"You got it," Nancy agreed. "I see you're feeling better today, Joe."

"I am, except that I hope none of what happened here last night gets into the papers. I was thinking that even if Roseanne is found innocent, the whole business might damage her career. I'd hate to see her hurt by all this."

"I understand." Nancy put her hand on his arm. "You don't have to say anything."

"You're okay, Drew," Joe returned. "Did I ever tell you that?"

"Coffee, Nancy?" Frank asked her.

"Tea."

"A tea, please," Frank called to the waitress. "Now. For today"—he pushed the pad toward Nancy—"the way I see it, all the early crimes, the dyed caviar, the rat in the restaurant, the jammed ski-lift, the fire in the blower system, were clearly acts of sabotage. But we don't know if that's true of the sawed-through skis, the switched trail markers, and the missing chemicals from the infirmary. And who knows where Lampley's death fits in?"

Nancy took Frank's list and read it over as the waitress set Nancy's tea on the table. "I still have a gnawing feeling there's a connection we're missing."

"Maybe so," Frank said, nodding. "But one thing's for sure. We've got one or more very active criminals here."

"Look who's here." Joe pointed to the door. Bess and George, looking alive if not fully awake, were threading their way to Nancy's table.

"Hello, everyone," a still sleepy Bess murmured, flopping down in her seat.

"Interesting weather we're having," George said.

"It's fate," Joe said.

"Food," Bess pleaded, rubbing her eyes.

"Hey, you made it, Bess. Good for you!" Nancy ribbed her friend.

"Yeah, yeah," Bess replied with a grin and a sigh.

"How's the wrist, George?" Frank asked.

"It'll feel all right when the aspirin I took kicks in," George assured her. "So, what's on for today? Do I get to tag along with Raven Maxwell again?"

"Yes, you do," Nancy confirmed. "What's on her agenda, do you know?"

"Well, the backup singers got here yesterday afternoon. She wanted to tape their segment, and I think she's going to shoot some dancing footage, too."

"And I guess Bess is back on Brad MacDougal duty," Frank concluded. "That leaves Ken. We really ought to keep an eye on his movements, too."

George looked surprised. "Frank, you don't really believe Ken—"

"Is guilty? No, not really," Frank told her. "But I do think he may be in danger."

Joe spoke up. "Say no more," he said, holding up his hand. "It's all taken care of. I can't follow Roseanne around all day, after all."

Nancy nodded, then turned to Frank. "I think you and I need to circulate around a bit," she said. I'd like another look at the videotape of last night."

"Right," Frank replied. "And we should look through some guest rooms, too—those stolen chemicals have to be somewhere."

"That reminds me!" Nancy blurted. "I completely forgot, with everything else that happened last night. I found something in Raven's room!" She told them about the letter she'd read.

"If she had a motive for the murder, maybe

she's trying to cover up by pointing the finger at Roseanne!" Joe said excitedly.

"We don't know that for sure, Joe," Nancy said, draining her tea. "But I plan on finding out. Keep that letter in mind, George, when you're watching Raven. Now, let's go, shall we?"

"Not until I get some breakfast in me," Bess said.

"Me, too," George chimed in.

"Catch you later," Nancy told them.

Nancy and the Hardys went their separate ways, with Nancy and Frank heading for the video screening room. Their route took them down the main hall and up the stairs to the second floor.

Outside, the storm howled. Snow was spiraling through the darkened sky, blowing in every direction with the thick gusts of wind. It didn't look as though it was going to stop any time soon, either.

"Hey, somebody left the window open!" Nancy said as they reached the landing. At their feet the floor was dusted with melting snow that had blown in from outside.

"Better give me a hand closing this thing," Frank called to her. "It's stuck."

Nancy leaned on the other end of the large window. She was about to push, when Frank suddenly put a finger to his lips. He pointed down, and Nancy heard people speaking outside, directly below them. An overhang in the roof prevented her from seeing who they were.

It was hard to make out any words. But one thing was perfectly clear—they were arguing, and one voice was hopping mad.

"More than we bargained for . . ." The words drifted up at them. "Going behind my back . . ." The howling wind took the rest of the words with it, and the other person's response was completely inaudible.

"I'd like to know who's out there in this weather, wouldn't you?" Frank asked.

"You bet!" Nancy replied.

"I better get what's coming to me, that's all I have to say. . . ." came the first voice, a gruff, masculine one whose pitch sounded familiar. "Or else you'll end up like that promoter . . ."

That promoter—they were talking about Archer Lampley!

Nancy and Frank leaned forward, straining to identify the voice.

"Remember what I said. . . ."

The voice became inaudible as the wind gusted. Still listening, Frank said quietly, "Recognize that voice, Nancy? We heard it on top of the hill yesterday."

Their eyes met. Nancy's widened in sudden recognition. "Pete Dawson!"

Chapter Fourteen

"HURRY, FRANK!" Nancy was already bounding down the stairs toward the fire exit. They pressed the lever to open the door as quietly as they could.

Outside, snow was still falling. There was an eerie silence, broken only by the howl of the wind.

They headed for the area outside the window. When they got there, it was deserted.

"Can you believe it?" Frank muttered. "Our big chance, and we blew it!"

"Not so fast!" Nancy said. "The stair door opens only from the inside. If they were going back in, they'd have to go around to the front."

She led Frank along the wall of the building. Suddenly he whistled and pointed down: two sets of footprints told them she was right. The footprints were sunk deep in the powder.

The prints led to the corner of the building, then went separate ways. Nancy turned to Frank. "Should we split up?"

He nodded. "I'll take these," he said, indicating the set of tracks that led away from the building.

"See you later, then!" Nancy trudged off after the other set of tracks but quickly saw that it was no use: they led her straight to the front entrance. Whoever had made those tracks had gone back inside and disappeared into the lodge. She turned around and doubled back.

At the corner she broke away from the wall of the building and took off after Frank. His was the only real set of tracks left to follow. The original set was now little more than a faint impression in the snow, blurred by the drifting powder.

The tracks led to the back of the lodge and up the mountain. They edged upward, then doubled back again. Nancy had no idea where she was heading. Because of the storm, she could see only two feet in front of her. Once the lights from the lodge faded, all she was aware of was the sea of white surrounding her.

How they would find their way down again

was anybody's guess, but right now she had to keep going.

"I better get what's coming to me or else you'll end up like that promoter. . . ." The words she and Frank had heard through the window set Nancy's mind in motion.

As she followed the tracks, Nancy thought hard. If Pete had been responsible for the sabotage, was somebody putting him up to it? Was the same pair involved in Archer's murder? Pete had been nowhere near the murder scene that fateful night. Could he still have been an accomplice? If so, whose? And why was Pete unhappy with the arrangement?

She wondered if the murder was somehow related to the small acts of sabotage. Something told Nancy there had to be a connection. It couldn't be just some sort of horrible coincidence.

Then it hit her. The common factor could be Pete Dawson. He could have been an accomplice to both the sabotage and the murder.

The snow battered Nancy's face, making her skin sting and her eyes water. Momentarily dizzy, she stumbled backward, then caught her breath and moved on. Frank's footsteps were fainter now, as the path became steeper and more slippery. How much farther can I go? Nancy wondered.

She trudged on, rounding a huge rock outcropping. Then the snow stopped for a moment, and Nancy caught a brief glimpse of the ski lift and, behind it, a ramshackle cabin. Pete Dawson's cabin.

Nancy drew in her breath. About a hundred feet in front of the cabin, hidden behind a tree, was Frank Hardy. She stumbled through the snow and, panting, came up beside him. "Hi," she whispered, touching her mittened hand to his shoulder.

Frank smiled with surprise and pleasure. "Fancy meeting you here. Any luck?" he asked.

"No. Whoever it was ducked inside the main lodge before I got there," Nancy said with a frown.

"Well, I saw Pete go inside, but I thought I'd wait awhile before I tried to get any closer. I was hoping you might show up."

"Well, here I am. Let's go."

The two detectives began to approach the cabin, using trees and boulders for cover as they edged closer. With all the snow, chances were slim that Pete would see them. Still, better to be safe, Nancy thought.

At Frank's signal, they made a dash for the window, coming to a stop right at the wall. Taking deep breaths, they exhaled away from the window so their breath wouldn't show.

"Okay," Frank mouthed soundlessly.

Nancy nodded back. They inched upward and peeked in through the corner of the window where it wasn't too fogged over. Pete Dawson was throwing a log on a fire that flickered in an old-fashioned hearth.

The sight of the fire made Nancy realize how cold she was. Her fingers, even in her mittens, had gone numb. She could hardly feel her toes anymore. If Dawson didn't do something incriminating soon, they'd either have to turn back or ask to be invited in!

As they waited, Nancy heard a faint rumbling from up the mountain. Tugging at her sleeve, Frank signaled Nancy to look inside the cabin. Pete Dawson was at the door, bolting it shut. As they watched, Pete went over to the far wall and pulled back a heavy curtain, revealing a crude but very well-stocked laboratory.

Pete rifled through the shelves, obviously looking for something. Finally he brought down a glass jar and opened it. He didn't seem to like what he saw. With a look of disgust, he threw on his coat and strapped on snowshoes. Then he unbolted the door and strode outside.

Nancy and Frank flattened themselves against the cabin wall as Pete marched out into the driving snow, not ten feet from them. He nearly turned in their direction but then, mumbling, walked off down the mountain.

Once Pete was well out of sight, Frank shouted, "Come on!" Nancy followed him as he dashed for the door. In another moment they were inside.

"Whew!" said Nancy, taking off her gloves. "Let me get over by this fire right away!"

"Brrrrrr." Frank shivered as he joined her at the fire, rubbing his frosty cheeks.

"Do you think we should have kept following him?" Nancy asked.

"Are you kidding? We'd have ended up as human icicles!" Frank said with a laugh. "It's cold out there!"

She nodded in agreement. Cold wasn't the word for it.

"Seriously, though, he's going to see his boss—I just know it. The one he argued with before."

"I came to the same conclusion myself." Frank nodded, his smile fading. "But, listen, we've got a few minutes before his tracks fade. Let's have a look around here."

"Good idea." Nancy rubbed her hands together in front of the fire. "As soon as my fingers thaw out."

Frank flexed his hands dramatically. "To work!" he announced, moving around the room. "Looks pretty normal, except for that chem lab."

"Let's have a look." Nancy walked over to the makeshift lab.

"Wow, this is a terrorist's dream!" she said,

pointing to the explosive charges, timers, fuses, detonators.

"Could be for mining," Frank pointed out. "Or sabotage," he concluded.

"I wonder if he has permits to buy all this stuff?"

"We'll have to check that out," Frank agreed.

"Here's some blue dye," Nancy said excitedly. "That could have been what was used on the caviar."

"Whoa! Here's the jar he looked so upset about!" Frank sniffed inside the empty glass jar, then let Nancy have a whiff, too. It smelled of bitter almonds.

"Cyanide," she said.

"Oh, boy. I think we've just saved Roseanne's neck," Frank said.

"Not so fast," Nancy reminded him. "She could be paying Pete off."

"Think so?" Frank asked.

"I don't know," she answered. "But that's what Sheriff Brady might say. Look, let's get out of here. We should follow Pete before his tracks get cold. He might be up to something at this very moment."

"You're right, Nancy." Frank picked up the jar and gave it to Nancy to put in her purse. She took a vial of the blue dye.

In a moment, they had collected all the evidence. They were pulling their mittens on, when suddenly Frank laid a hand on Nancy's arm.

"Listen," he said. It was the rumbling sound they'd heard before, but now it was a lot louder and closer.

Nancy ran to the window and looked outside. The storm had eased up, but the rumbling was getting deeper now, shaking the rickety house.

Then she saw it—a wall of snow heading down the mountain, right for them!

Chapter Fifteen

"IT'S AN AVALANCHE!" Nancy cried.

"Take cover, quick!" In a flash, Frank grabbed Nancy and pushed her under the kitchen table. He ducked in next to her and crouched down. "If the house is hit, we'll need every bit of protection we can get."

"I know." Nancy nodded. "Frank, do you really think—" But her words were drowned out. The rumble became a thunderous roar.

"We're in for it, Nan!"

The window burst into a thousand pieces as the avalanche went thundering past, shaking the cabin to its foundation.

Nancy looked up at the wavering ceiling and

prayed the roof would hold. Pieces of plaster dropped to the floor and smashed against the tabletop.

Overhead, the light fixture began swinging wildly. It crashed to the floor beside them, sending broken glass spraying in all directions.

But the roof held, and at last the shaking stopped. A chilling silence filled the cabin, now dark except for the dim light from the dying fire.

Nancy and Frank stumbled out from under the rickety table and stood up, surveying the damage.

"Wow," Frank said quietly. "I don't find too many things scary, but that was *scary.*"

Nancy walked to the bathroom and tried flicking on the light. "No light here, either," she said. "The power lines must have been knocked out." She went to the door and tried opening it, but the snow had blocked them in.

"It's no use," she said, closing the door with a frown. "We'll never be able to dig our way out of that."

The hole that was once a window was also blocked by a huge mass of snow. "Looks like we're stuck here for a while," Frank said. He forced a smile.

"I guess so," Nancy said, biting her lip and looking around for a possible exit.

"So—what do we do now?" Frank moved around the cabin, examining the damage.

"The roof has got to be buried," Nancy murmured. "The fire is dying, and that's a sure sign of a blocked chimney."

"Forget leaving by the door or the window," Frank said with a sigh. "We stay until they dig us out, I guess."

Shaking her head in disbelief, Nancy went over to the smoldering fire. The force of the snowslide had blown cinders everywhere, and she stamped out the ones that were still burning.

"I think a new fire would be a good idea, even if it doesn't last very long," she said. But after looking for logs to replenish the fire, she quickly realized that the one Pete had thrown on the fire earlier must have been the last.

"He must keep the logs outside," Frank said ruefully.

There wasn't even a twig left in the small cabin. Nancy looked at the lone chair and table in the room. Metal. Terrific.

She studied the lab shelves. They were made of metal, too. The closet didn't have a door, just a curtain draped in front of it. The bed was only a mattress on the floor. In the whole cabin, there wasn't a single thing to burn.

Even if anyone thought to dig them out, it would probably be a day or two before they were rescued. They could easily freeze before anyone even knew they were missing!

Nancy looked over at Frank and saw that he was thinking the very same thing. Their eyes locked and then turned away. Neither of them wanted to voice such a terrible thought.

There was a stunning silence in the cabin. The smoldering fire glowed faintly, but it wasn't giving a shred of real heat.

"So here we are." Frank managed to smile at her, then sighed heavily. He stared into the fireplace, the orange light bathing his handsome features with an eerie glow.

"For better or worse." Nancy went over and stood next to him, watching the fire die.

Frank turned and looked deeply in her eyes. "If this is it, Nancy," he said softly, "I just want you to know that—well—"

"Oh, Frank, don't talk like that. We'll get through this somehow." He was looking right through her, and in spite of the danger, Nancy felt that feeling again—that awful-wonderful rush she often felt when she was alone with Frank.

The two of them stood staring at each other for what seemed to Nancy like ages. With a cough, she tried to break the spell. "Come on, now. We're not through yet. I don't know how, but we're going to make it. We've just got to concentrate on surviving."

She walked over to the bed, quickly stripping off the threadbare blankets. "Here. Maybe it'll help if we wrap ourselves in these," she suggested, shivering slightly.

"You're shaking," Frank said, opening his arms. He wrapped her in the blankets and pulled her against his chest.

Nancy huddled against him, pressing closer. Frank was so warm, so full of life. She couldn't bear the thought that this might be the end.

"Any better?" Frank asked, his breath warm on her face.

"A little," she replied through chattering teeth.

He held her close and stroked her hair. A warm rush went through Nancy. For one brief moment, the cold was behind them. They stood pressed against each other, nestling in the other's warmth.

The fire faded into blackness, and the room grew even colder. Frank took his arm from around Nancy's back and reached down to touch her face. She lifted her head. She saw the intense longing in his eyes. She closed her eyes and felt the power of her feelings overwhelm her. Her head was spinning with cold, fear, and longing.

In a desperate, wonderful moment, their lips met.

Joe and Roseanne arrived at the disco to find Raven showing George the ropes. She was explaining how to shoot from several angles at once. At the same time, she was telling the crew how to set up the disco for the next shot.

"That woman is incredible," Joe whispered to Roseanne. "I don't know how she does it."

"It's her job, that's all." In her makeup and costume, Roseanne looked radiant, but all the signs of tension were there. As she stepped onto the stage, she kept looking over at Joe as if for moral support. Once again, his heart went out to her.

"Hi, everybody!" Bess burst in, holding Brad's hand. Joe could tell Brad was getting a little tired of Bess.

"Hi, all," Brad said wearily. "Where's Raven?"

"Right here," Raven piped up from behind a huge camera. As usual, she had a pencil over her ear and a clipboard in hand.

"Say, Raven." Brad turned to her. "I'd like to have a word with you, in private, if you don't mind."

Raven looked around, then checked her watch. "Well, the lighting men are setting up. I suppose now's as good a time as any. But only five minutes, okay?"

"Two minutes. Just two." Brad led Raven outside. He held on to her arm as she stepped over the miles of cable lying around the room.

Bess pouted. "Boy. I don't know what's

going on with Brad today," she told George and Joe. "He's acting really strange."

"Speaking of strange, has either of you seen Nancy or Frank?" Joe asked. "They've been gone all day. I'm starting to worry about them."

"Oh, don't worry about those two." Bess smiled mischievously. "They can take care of themselves."

"Come on, Bess," George put in. "This is no time for jokes. You know Frank and Nancy are all business, especially when they're in the middle of a case."

"That's true," Joe said doubtfully, remembering the scene he'd witnessed the night before.

"I think we ought to look for them," George said, interrupting his thoughts. "What do you say we make a quick search of the main lodge?"

"Okay by me," Joe agreed.

"Oh, all right. Brad can wait for me for once," Bess said, looking miffed.

As the three made their way to the exit, there was a sudden surge in the lights.

"Wow!" Bess cried, with an astonished smile. For a second the disco was brighter than a shooting star.

But Joe saw a startled look on one of the lighting men's faces. "Who's doing that? It's dangerous!" he shouted, his face washed out by the brightness.

"It's starting to hurt my eyes!" Bess shouted, as the brightness grew unbearable.

Suddenly there was a huge explosion—and the whole room went black.

Chapter Sixteen

"Look out!" Panicked voices shot through the dark disco, followed by a crash and then the sound of shattering glass. Joe guessed someone must have knocked over one of the huge spotlights in the dark.

"What's happening here, people?" Raven shouted above the noise, her voice unnaturally high and shrill.

"It isn't our lighting system, Raven," someone answered. "It must be some sort of general blackout."

"Joe! Where are you?" Roseanne's voice was right nearby. There was an edge of desperation to it.

"I'm coming. Don't move." In the pitch-black, he found Roseanne's hand and gave it a squeeze. "Are you okay?" he asked.

"I think so. I can't see you at all," Roseanne answered, her voice wavering. She was gripping his hand for dear life.

"Come on!" he cried. "We're getting out of here. Bess, take my other hand." He groped in the darkness for Bess's hand.

"Come on, George," Bess said.

"Let's go, then." Feeling along the wall of the room, Joe made his way to the double-door exit. The corridor was just as dark as the disco. The whole lodge was blacked out. Joe knew they'd have to reach the fireplace in the grand lobby in order to have light. Cautiously, he guided the girls down the corridor until they saw the faint glow of the fire.

"I hear people!" Roseanne said hopefully. "We must be near the fireplace." A glow of light welcomed them. Several guests were standing around, speculating about the cause of the blackout. Nobody seemed to really know the reason.

"Ken!" Joe called out. He spotted the lodge's owner peering down an empty corridor from the central lobby.

"I hope everyone is all right," Ken murmured as more guests trickled into the area. "Where were you when it happened?"

"The disco," Bess answered. "We left the

crew there, fumbling around in the dark. I hope they're okay."

"Ken, could you stay here with Bess and Roseanne?" Joe broke in. "I want to check out the generator."

"Don't bother, Joe. I've just come from there." Ken ran a nervous hand through his hair. "The generator leads have been completely destroyed. And the auxiliary generator was smashed."

"Then it was sabotage!" Joe stared back at him.

Ken just nodded and sighed. "From the job that someone did, it looks like Mount Mirage will be in the dark for days."

The cold was beginning to make Nancy feel weak—or maybe it was Frank Hardy's kiss. She looked up at the ceiling. The entire room seemed to be floating around her. Shaking herself back to reality, Nancy put her hands over her eyes and squeezed them shut. She sat up. Pull yourself together, she said silently.

Frank was lying on his side, his eyes open. He hadn't spoken for a long time. "Frank?" she said.

"Mmmm . . ." He was awake, if not exactly alert.

"I think we'd better keep talking."

"Okay," he replied wearily. He pulled himself up to a sitting position and drew the blanket around them both.

"I think I've been hallucinating. I thought the room was spinning," Nancy confessed in a hoarse whisper.

"Funny. I did, too."

Frank's saying that scared her. Maybe they were both going crazy from the cold.

"But, Nancy, I don't think I'm imagining this." His voice was stronger this time. "The floor is moving!" He pointed behind her, by the kitchen table.

Nancy shook her head. "I don't think so, Frank."

"It is!" Frank's voice was insistent. "I swear it's moving, Nan! Look!"

Nancy squeezed her eyes shut, then opened them quickly and turned to look in the direction where Frank was pointing. He was right! The floor in the middle of the room was moving. Nancy saw a rectangular bulge take shape under the frayed carpet.

The bulge grew larger, then the carpet was thrown back. There was a trapdoor under the rug! Nancy and Frank looked on in amazement as Pete Dawson emerged. He was carrying a brightly lit hurricane lamp in his right hand and wearing a scowl on his face.

Nancy put a hand over her eyes to help adjust them to the sudden infusion of light.

Dawson caught the shadow of her movement flickering on the wall and turned in surprise. "What—"

He held up the lantern. By its light he could see Nancy and Frank huddled together under the blankets.

"What are you doing here?" he growled menacingly.

Nancy blinked, her eyes still hurting from the glare of the lantern. She had to think fast. "We got stranded out in the storm," she explained. "And we saw the cabin—"

"We needed to get out of the storm," Frank took up the story. "Then we got—well, buried, and there wasn't any way out." He put his arm around Nancy. "We decided to make the best of a bad situation." He winked at Pete mischievously and gave Nancy's shoulders a squeeze.

Pete looked from Frank to Nancy and back again. Then he slowly broke into a nasty little smile. "Sure, I get you. A little romance, huh?"

Then his smile vanished abruptly. "You're those two detectives, aren't you?" he said. "You were snooping around here, right?"

"You've got it wrong. When the police came, they took us off the case." Frank's explanation sounded pretty convincing.

"Then what were you doing out in the storm?" Pete said angrily. "Taking a pleasure stroll?" He looked up at his lab, went over, and pulled back the curtain. "At least you didn't leave a mess," Pete said.

Nancy swallowed hard. They'd managed to put the evidence in her purse before he'd arrived!

Pete turned back to them. "You think I killed that Lampley guy, don't you?" Pete said abruptly. There was an edge of fear in his voice. "I know you do. Well, I didn't. I was nowhere near him. I don't mess with murder, understand? I'm not a killer."

Nancy and Frank shot each other a furtive glance. It was now or never.

"Pete," Nancy said, "we know you didn't kill Archer Lampley. We can prove it. Frank saw you that night, far away from the scene of the crime. If we get out of here, we can clear your name with the police."

Dawson seemed confused. "Someone stole the cyanide from me," he said. "I only found out today."

"Do you have any idea who took it?" Frank prodded.

Dawson laughed. "Do I have any idea? You bet your life I do."

"Tell us!" Nancy pleaded. "We can help you, Pete, but only if you come clean with us."

Pete gave her a hopeful look, and for a moment she thought he would talk. Then he straightened up and glared at them. "Just stay out of my way, all right? I'm going to handle this thing my way. I'll point you back to the lodge, and you can call the police. Just tell them Pete Dawson is innocent of murder. I'll take care of everything else."

He went over to the open trapdoor and held up his lantern. "Follow me," he said, starting down the ladder.

A rickety wooden ladder led them about twenty feet down into an old mine shaft. There was no rail spur, only a narrow tunnel leading off in either direction. The tunnel was braced by crude wooden beams.

"My father dug this pit, and I added to it," Pete told them as they walked. "It should have made us rich, but it never did. This is Mount Mirage, all right. No gold, no nothing."

Nancy looked at Pete's back as they bent to avoid hitting the tunnel's roof. His posture betrayed a life spent hacking at the rock walls of his father's barren dream. No wonder he was so bitter.

After about a hundred feet, the tunnel ended. Pete opened a rough wooden door at the tunnel's end. Nancy and Frank emerged into the cold night. It had stopped snowing, but the wind was still howling under the slate-gray sky.

"Just head that way for about two hundred yards," Dawson told them. "You'll end up at the snowmobile garage. You can find your way from there." Pete turned and started back into the tunnel. "You just call the cops and tell them I'm innocent," he called back before the door snapped shut.

Nancy and Frank followed Pete's directions, feeling their way as they went. It was a slow, tortuous route in the deep snow, but Nancy felt great just to be alive.

"Wow!" Frank exulted as they went. "Do you realize that not only did we get out of there alive, but we practically solved the case? The blue dye proves that Pete is our saboteur. And he seems to know who stole his cyanide, too. There's got to be a way to get him to talk!"

"I'm not sure there is, Frank," Nancy said cautiously. As much as she wanted to feel confident, she wasn't sure the case was in the bag.

A few hundred yards down the slope they came to the snowmobile garage. Beyond it loomed the great black bulk of the main building. "Hey," Frank said, coming to a halt in front of her. "The lights are out!"

"Looks like a total blackout," Nancy agreed, glancing around her. "We can call the police from the phones in front of the lobby."

They tramped through the drifts surrounding the building and fought their way to the front entrance. Panting for breath, they ran to the outdoor phones.

"Great!" Frank said, picking up a receiver. He started dialing, then stopped, and lowered the phone.

"No luck?" Nancy asked, pushing her hands deep into her pockets.

Frank shook his head and reached for another phone. And another. And another.

"All the phones are dead, Nancy," he said at last. "The lines must be down!"

Chapter Seventeen

WHEN FRANK AND NANCY walked into the main lobby, they were greeted by the sight of the whole hotel camped out. Kerosene lamps cast friendly pools of light that drew the two of them forward.

Crew members, backup vocalists, instrumentalists, Worldwide Children's Charities donors, guests, and staffers were spread out in front of the fireplace and around the lamps in little knots, conversing, complaining, and sharing stories.

Frank saw Ken looking very rumpled and tired, as were a lot of the others.

"Nancy! Frank!" George sprang up from the

sofa the minute she saw her friends approach. "Thank goodness you're back! We were worried."

"Where were you?" cried Bess, gripping Nancy by the arm and pulling her to where she and George were sitting. "We were all so worried!"

Frank glanced at Nancy. "It's a long story, guys," Nancy said, walking them over to a more private spot.

"We made some real headway today," Frank added.

"Really? That's great," Bess said.

"Hey, hey! Look who's here!" A jubilant Joe stepped over to them, reaching out for Frank's hand and pulling him in for a hug.

"Hi, Joe," Frank said, thumping his brother's back in response.

"They found something!" Bess told Joe.

Joe's eyes lit up. "Have we got our man yet?"

"Not yet," Frank answered, "but we're getting close. For instance, we know the blue dye Ken was telling us about came from Pete Dawson. And it seems some cyanide was stolen from him, too."

"Good work," Joe said.

"Pete's definitely working with an accomplice," Nancy added. "We heard the two of them talking, but we didn't find out who the other person was."

"What's been happening around here?"

Frank broke in. "The phone lines are all dead."

"Not only that, the generator leads were blasted to smithereens," Joe said.

"What?" Frank exclaimed.

"I went down to the generator room to check it out. There's nothing left to see," Joe said. "The whole thing was blown to bits with plastic explosives."

Frank's jaw tightened. "There were explosives like that in Pete's cabin."

"But we don't think Pete killed Archer Lampley," Nancy threw in.

"He wasn't at the lodge, for starters," Frank agreed.

"Did you happen to notice a miniature hacksaw at his cabin?" George asked. "Maybe he was the one who sawed through the skis."

"It's there," Nancy said with a nod. Frank looked surprised. "I noticed it when we were looking for firewood, but I forgot to tell you," she added softly.

"So what do we do now?" Bess wondered, looking from Nancy to Frank.

"Get the police," Frank answered.

"But how?"

"I could hop on a snowmobile," Joe offered.

"There was a blizzard out there, Joe! It's too dark, too windy, and too dangerous," Frank told him.

"But if he's guilty, Pete could be trying to

escape right now!" Joe protested. "I could find my way to town!"

"Sorry, Joe. I can't let you." The serious tone in his brother's voice told Joe that Frank meant business.

"Here you are, folks! Get 'em while they're hot!" Frank spun around and saw Chester Peabody and his wife, holding out separate skewers of miniature hot dogs. "Go ahead, there are plenty for everyone."

"The wieners are just going to go bad if we don't eat them," Pearl added. "The kitchen's trying to get rid of them."

"Thanks," Frank said, taking a couple of hot dogs hungrily. "Nancy?"

With a nod of thanks to the Peabodys, Nancy helped herself.

"Is everyone okay?" Ken approached the group, his hands in his pockets.

"What's the story with the lights?" Pearl asked him. "When can we expect 'em back on?"

Ken looked embarrassed but tried to cover his discomfort. "It may be a while, Mrs. Peabody. I'm terribly sorry. I hope you'll—"

"You know, I could probably rig up something in about an hour or so. Would you like me to try?" Chester offered.

"Are you joking, Mr. Peabody?" Ken asked. "Maybe you didn't hear me say the generator leads were gone—completely blown away."

"No problem," Chester said, handing his hot dog to his wife. "I'm saying you can bypass the leads, if you arrange a few other things differently. See, here . . ."

He began explaining, drawing in the air with his fingers. It was totally unintelligible even to Frank, who knew a thing or two about circuitry. Still, Chester sounded as if he knew what he was doing.

"Mr. Peabody, what about the phones? Any chance we can get them working first?" Frank asked.

The inventor smiled. "Afraid I don't know much about phones, son," he told Frank. "If you have a call to make—use my car phone."

Frank threw his arm around the surprised inventor. "Mr. Peabody," he said, "you're not only a genius, you're a lifesaver!"

Within a few minutes Joe had led Chester, Peabody, and Frank down to the generator room. Pearl Peabody went with Nancy into the lodge's parking lot to point her in the direction of Chester's car.

"I'd go with you, honey," Pearl said, "but I don't really like the cold. You understand, don't you?" Nancy smiled. "The door's open, anyway," Pearl added. "Good luck." She walked back inside the lodge on her spiked high heels.

Nancy made her way across the parking lot to where Chester Peabody's green Mercedes was parked. In a few seconds, she was sitting in the driver's seat, the car phone in her hand. She dialed the sheriff's number. After three rings, she heard, "Sheriff Brady speaking."

"Sheriff, it's Nancy Drew up at Mount Mirage Lodge and Villas."

"I remember you," he said, his voice dripping with contempt. "Sorry I couldn't make it out there today, but you may have noticed we had a little snow."

"You've got to come to the lodge," Nancy said, ignoring the sarcasm. "There's been more sabotage. The power's out, and the phone lines are down. I'm talking on a car phone now. And we have something we know you'll be interested in."

"Oh, yeah? What's that?"

"An accomplice to murder."

There was a long silence on Brady's end, then he said, "You sure? It only takes one hand to dose a drink with cyanide, you know."

"There's more to it than that," Nancy replied.

"All right, tell me about it."

"I will. When you get here."

It took a long moment for Brady to respond, and when he did, he didn't sound pleased. "Do you realize we just had three feet of snow, young lady? The roads are all blocked!"

"Don't you have a helicopter?" Nancy asked.

"Of course we have a helicopter!" he boomed back.

"Sheriff, there's a murderer on the loose up here. Somebody could be seriously hurt if you don't come."

"I'll be there by dawn, young lady, and no sooner."

Nancy hung up and started back to rejoin the others. As she approached the lodge, the lights came on. Good old Chester! she thought to herself. He did know what he was talking about.

Back in the main lobby, Jack Treyford was leading the celebration. "Good work, Peabody!" he shouted when Chester returned. "Harrison, I don't know what to say—having *guests* fix the power lines. Listen, everyone, I'm going to throw a party at my villa tomorrow evening at eight. I have my own generator, so you can rely on having light." He laughed, and quite a few people in the room laughed along with him.

But Ken Harrison wasn't laughing. "I can't stand that man," he whispered to Nancy when she came up beside him.

Nancy told Ken about her phone call to the sheriff. He looked relieved. "I'm going up to my room, everybody," she said. "I'm bushed. See you in the morning."

"Good night, Nancy," Frank said.

"We'll be up soon," George added. "I promised Bess I'd wait for her to say good night to Brad."

With a wave to her friends, Nancy made her way back to her room.

As she got ready for bed, the nagging worry at the back of her mind came forward. What exactly was happening between her and Frank Hardy? It seemed as if one tiny spark of attraction was heating up to a fire, and it didn't feel right at all. Frank Hardy was a great guy, but he wasn't Ned.

Nancy flicked off the light beside her bed. If only she and Ned weren't apart so much. If only he could be there, if only he hadn't had to study. Oh, Ned, she said silently, staring out into the darkness. Where are you when I need you?

With a sigh, she reached for the pull to shut the curtains, then paused for a moment. Something was moving out there on the ski slope. One of the ski gondolas was gently swinging back and forth.

Could the lift have been started by accident, she wondered, when the power was restored?

She hoped that was the explanation. Because there was nothing more she could do that night—except sleep.

The next morning dawned clear and cold. Nancy glanced over at the sleeping forms of

Bess and George as a ray of brilliant sunlight peeked through under the edge of the curtain.

Getting out of bed, she went straight to the window and pulled the curtain open. The sun sparkled off the heaps of fresh snow on the mountain, momentarily blinding her. As her eyes adjusted, she glanced at the lift she'd thought she'd seen moving the night before. It was still now, and for one sleepy moment she wondered if she'd only imagined it moving.

By six-thirty Nancy, Frank, and Joe were down in front of the lodge along with Ken Harrison, watching the police helicopter land. Sheriff Brady stepped out, accompanied by three other police officers.

"All right, we're here. What's the story?" he asked.

Frank and Nancy told them about their encounter with Pete Dawson. Sheriff Brady agreed that they should go up and confront Dawson as soon as possible.

"There's a trail to Pete's cabin, but it's under several feet of snow," Frank told him. "I suggest we take the gondola to the top of the slopes and ski to the cabin."

"Ski down?" Brady repeated faintly.

"You do ski, don't you, Sheriff?" Nancy asked. "It's a fairly easy run."

Brady snorted. "Lead the way," he ordered gruffly.

While they strapped on their skis, Ken turned on the gondola lift. They boarded and began riding up the mountain.

Halfway up, Nancy caught sight of a figure in one of the descending chairs. "Somebody's in that chair," she told the others.

"Who could it be at this hour?" Ken asked, leaning over to get a better look. "The lifts aren't usually running this early."

Nancy peered over as the chair swung past them. The man inside was slumped over, and he wasn't moving.

"It's Pete Dawson!" she cried out. "And he looks dead!"

Chapter Eighteen

"SHOT IN THE SIDE," Joe heard the portly forensics man tell Sheriff Brady. They were all standing outside the lodge by the foot of the ski lift. "It's a little hard to tell when, since the body's been out in the cold."

Nancy stood next to Joe, listening intently. Frank, in the meantime, was examining the lift.

"Any ballistics information?" Sheriff Brady asked the forensics man.

"It was a twenty-two caliber, fired at close range—one foot or less. There are powder burns all around the hole in his jacket."

"Whew." Sheriff Brady winced and shook his head. He turned to Nancy and Joe. "Anything to add?"

"When I went to bed last night, I looked out my window and thought I saw a chair moving," Nancy told the sheriff. "I don't understand, though."

"Now," Brady addressed the teenagers, a superior look on his face, "would you like *me* to tell you what happened?"

"Sure, Sheriff," Joe said. "Go ahead and tell us."

"The killer comes to Mount Mirage intending to shoot Archer Lampley. Then he or she discovers that Pete keeps cyanide around. Now the killer decides that poison's a better way to go. By the way," he added with a nod to them, "thanks for telling me about the cyanide in Pete's cabin. Anyway, the killer buys, borrows, or steals the cyanide and commits the murder in the hopes that the death will pass for a heart attack. She, or he, doesn't count on the police detecting cyanide. After all, why would they even be looking for poison?"

Joe's face grew red. "I don't like where you're taking this," he growled.

"But," the sheriff went on, ignoring Joe, "when the killer realizes she's a suspect in Lampley's death, she gets scared and decides to get rid of Pete right away. She invites him for a ride on the lift, offering money or other inducements. Then she shoots him and dumps the gun in the snow. The end."

He looked at them smugly. "What do you think?" he asked Nancy. Before she could answer, he turned to Joe. "I already know what *you* think."

"Why don't you just come out and say you think Roseanne James did it?" Joe asked, struggling to keep his temper.

"Well, I do have my suspicions," Brady admitted.

Joe was about to unleash his opinion of Sheriff Brady's suspicions when his brother returned. Reading the situation, Frank put a calming arm on Joe's shoulder.

"She came to Mount Mirage with a twenty-two caliber pistol. You can't deny that," Brady asserted. "Now she claims it was stolen."

"It *was* stolen!" Joe protested.

"Sheriff," Nancy broke in urgently, "do you really believe Roseanne would have left the empty vial of cyanide under her own pillow if she were the murderer?"

"Well," Brady replied with a shrug, "murderers do make mistakes. Especially murderers with no experience."

A policeman on skis came up to him. "I think you should take a look at this, Sheriff," he said.

Joe started violently. The officer was holding Roseanne's pearl-handled revolver!

"We found it at the top of the mountain, lying there in the snow. It wasn't buried or anything. Almost like it was put there for us to find."

Joe couldn't take it any longer. "You idiot!" he exploded. "That's exactly right. It *was* put there—just like the cyanide! Somebody's trying to implicate Roseanne!"

"Oh?" Brady asked. "And why would someone do that?"

"Because it's easy!" Joe said. "Because it's convenient!"

Brady wasn't giving an inch. "I'm having Ms. James taken in for questioning. One more word out of you and you can join her, understand?"

Joe was about to answer when he felt Frank gripping his shoulder.

"Keep a lid on it, Joe," Frank said. "We need you."

"You have the right idea," Brady told Frank, "keeping that brother of yours in line. I'll talk to you all later," he said as he entered the lodge.

"Let's get moving," Joe said, angry and determined. "I want to take a look at those videotapes. They're all we have to go on right now."

"There's nothing on them, Joe, we've already looked," Frank assured him.

"*I* haven't looked," he answered.

"All right," Frank agreed. "We'll ask Raven to set up the machines."

"I want to get Bess and George first. They're probably up by now," Nancy put in. "I'd like them to watch Brad and Raven while we view the tapes. You never can tell what might be going on while we're busy."

"Good," Frank agreed. "Let's meet at the control booth."

When Nancy reached the door to her room a few minutes later, Bess and George were just coming out. They still looked a little sleepy.

"I'm afraid I have bad news," Nancy told them.

"What's wrong, Nancy?" George asked. "Did something happen?"

Nancy nodded. "Pete Dawson was murdered during the night, and the police are taking Roseanne James in for questioning."

"Oh, no!" Bess said with a gasp.

"I can't believe it," said George, shaking her head. "Another murder! What's going on?"

"We're going to have another look at the videotapes of Archer's death," Nancy explained. "I want you to come along and keep an eye on Raven and Brad, okay?"

"No problem," said George, game as always. Nancy gave her a grateful smile.

They made their way downstairs to where

the control booth was still set up. It was a good bet Raven would be there, planning her schedule for the day.

As soon as she pulled open the door to the soundstage, Nancy let out a gasp. In the far corner she saw Raven and Brad MacDougal, their arms wrapped around each other. They were sharing a long and passionate kiss!

Bess stiffened. "I can't believe this," she whispered. Tears rolling down her face, she ran back out into the hall.

"I'll go see if she's okay," Nancy told George. "Why don't you keep an eye on them and wait for Frank and Joe."

Nancy caught up with her friend in the ladies' room. "Oh, Bess," she said, hugging her. "I'm so sorry."

"I thought he liked me, Nancy," Bess sobbed. "He told me he cared about me, but now I see I'm just another star-struck girl to him. Ooohhh." And she was off again.

"Where's your makeup?" Nancy asked, all business. "You can't let him see you like this, Bess!"

Nancy had known Bess a long time, and she knew just how to get her friend back on her feet when a boy broke her heart.

Sure enough, Bess's disappointment and hurt quickly turned to angry determination. She reached purposefully into her bag and came up with her makeup kit. "Here!" she said, pushing it into Nancy's hands. "Make me gorgeous."

"You already are gorgeous." Nancy smiled. "Just stop crying, okay? It's not good for your mascara. Hold still and I'll touch it up."

When Nancy had finished, the effects were devastating. "You know, I don't look half bad," Bess remarked, studying herself in the mirror. "And I'll bet Brad was just buttering Raven up. After all, she's a big producer now."

Nancy smiled at her friend admiringly. Bess bruised easily, but she healed quickly, too.

"Now get back in there and show that rat he never meant a thing to you!" Nancy advised with a grin. "I'll meet you in a minute."

After Bess had gone, Nancy looked at herself in the mirror. Seeing Raven and Brad kissing had made her feel troubled again. There's a big difference between true love and flirting, Nancy thought with a sigh. That kiss she and Frank had shared had been wrong. Ned was the one she loved, she knew that now.

She had to tell Frank quickly, before things got out of hand and ruined their friendship, to say nothing of their working relationship. She should be concentrating on only one thing.

On her way back to the soundstage, Nancy ran into Frank in the hallway.

"Bess told me you'd be coming this way," he said. "I wanted to talk to you."

"Frank, there's something—"

"I have to say this right away, Nancy," he interrupted her. "It's very important."

"Wait, Frank, I have to tell you something first—"

Frank waved her off. "Nancy, about what happened yesterday. It can't ever happen again."

Nancy was struck dumb. Those were the very words she'd been about to say!

"I'm in love with Callie, Nancy. I feel terrible about what happened, because I really like you, but—"

"It's okay, Frank," Nancy broke in with a relieved smile. "I can't believe you're saying this, because I was just about to tell you that I'm in love with Ned!"

"You mean it?" he said hopefully.

"Uh-huh. But you don't have to look so thrilled!"

The two of them burst into relieved laughter. Once again, Nancy thought, their hearts and minds had run on parallel tracks.

Feeling whole again, she looked up at her friend and sighed. "Frank, you're the greatest."

In response, he put his arms around her and enveloped her in a warm hug. Oh, that feels so much better! she thought. She found herself breathing freely again.

"Well, don't let me interrupt!" a deep, familiar voice behind her spoke up. Nancy froze in midembrace. She spun around, still in Frank's arms. There, with an overnight bag slung on his shoulder, stood Ned Nickerson!

Chapter Nineteen

NANCY JERKED AWAY from Frank Hardy as though she'd been shot through with electricity. One hand flew to her neck, the other brushed back her hair.

"Ned!" she gasped, not knowing what to say. Ned's brown hair was tousled, and he looked so sweet. He was even wearing the sweater she'd given him for the holidays. "You're here!"

Ned looked from Nancy to Frank and back again, a troubled look in his beautiful brown eyes. He obviously didn't know what to make of seeing her in somebody else's arms. She could hardly blame him!

"Yeah. I, um, finished my studying and flew in last night. A police helicopter gave me a lift," he explained quietly, putting down his bag.

"Oh, Ned!" Nancy threw her arms around him and gave him a giant hug. "I'm so glad to see you!"

Pressing her face against his strong shoulder, she breathed in his delicious, familiar scent. Only Ned, she thought. What other boy would fly in to see her the day after a major blizzard?

He was hugging her back, but she could tell he was holding some affection in reserve. He clasped his hands awkwardly on her shoulders and let her kiss his cheek. Then he leaned toward Frank and held out his hand.

"Hi, Frank," he said. "I didn't know you were here."

"It was a last-minute thing," Frank explained awkwardly, taking Ned's outstretched hand and shaking it. "Joe's here, too."

"Well, that's good," Ned said after a pause. "Maybe I can pay you back for the help you gave me last time I saw you."

Good old Ned, Nancy thought. He was giving her and Frank the benefit of the doubt. Nancy slipped her arm through his and gave it a warm squeeze. He was her guy, all right. How could she have ever thought otherwise?

"Your being here is a real boost, Ned," Frank was saying now. "This one has us all stumped. The case started small, but things have escalated. Nancy'll fill you in. Now I'd better get out of here and help them cue up the tape. It may take a while. There's a lot of footage to look over," Frank said, excusing himself.

The minute Frank left, a silent tension crept over Ned and Nancy. Ned tightened when Nancy put her arm around his waist. No matter how gracious he'd just been to Frank Hardy, she could tell he was upset by seeing her with her arms around another guy.

"Well, you must be hungry. Let's go," she said. "We'll get some breakfast. We've got some time."

"Okay," he agreed. They began walking toward the restaurant elevator. Nancy's mind was racing. Obviously she ought to explain the encounter with Frank, but where to begin?

Before she could say anything, Ned reached around her waist and drew her to him affectionately. "Did you forget I might come?" he asked gently.

"Of course not!" Nancy gasped.

"Don't be so shocked. I'm only kidding," he said with a grin, ruffling her hair.

But once they settled into their booth at the restaurant and had given the waitress their order, Ned's face took on a serious look. "Nancy," he said, searching her eyes with his.

"Is there anything you want to tell me? Not about the case. About you."

"Ned, I—"

"Wait a minute, stop right there. What am I doing?" Ned looked down at the table and seemed to struggle for the right words. "Listen, you don't have to explain anything. I know you, but I don't own you, and I've never asked you to tie yourself to me. I know we're still pretty young, and we are apart a lot."

Feeling a lump in her throat, Nancy tried to interrupt. But Ned went on. "I'd understand if—I mean, I'd be upset, but I wouldn't have any right to be angry if you wanted to see other guys."

Ned was obviously sincere, but Nancy could see the hurt in his face.

"Oh, Ned!" She'd never meant to hurt him! How could she ever explain what had happened between her and Frank? Would he really understand?

He looked at her and sighed. "How about this? Just tell me if I should ever be worried," he said finally. He reached for her hand, and a bolt of love and affection shot right through Nancy.

"There's nothing for you to worry about," she said decisively, giving his strong hand a squeeze. "The beginning, middle, and end of it is that I'm crazy about you."

Ned smiled and relaxed in his chair. "So, what I saw when I came in . . . ?"

"Was nothing. Frank and I work together, and that kind of thing brings two people closer. But the truth is, I love you. Frank's a good friend, but you're the only one for me." It was truer than ever, Nancy realized. Just looking at Ned across the table made her heart beat triple time.

There *was* a little more to it than that, of course. Nancy couldn't deny that she was attracted to Frank Hardy. Being here with him at Mount Mirage had convinced her that the tiny *ping* she felt when she was around him would never go away.

But the bottom line was she didn't want to do anything about the *ping*. She finally knew that she could be friends with Frank and still be true to Ned.

And that's the way it was going to be from then on, she vowed. No way would she ever risk hurting Ned's feelings again. Not when she felt about him the way she did. What she had with Ned was a whole lot deeper than any *ping*.

"I really do love you, Ned." With a sigh, Nancy looked over at her boyfriend, and the warmth in his eyes melted her inhibitions. Their hands held harder, and their faces came closer until their lips were about to meet in a kiss.

"Western omelet?" The waitress's voice pulled them apart. "Eggs over easy?"

Ned smiled ruefully and gave Nancy a little wink. The spell was broken, for now at least.

"I ordered the eggs over easy," Nancy said, and the waitress set down their plates.

"Tell me about this case of yours," Ned prompted her. "The news said Archer Lampley died."

"Did it say he was murdered?" Nancy asked.

Ned was surprised. "Only that the police were investigating the cause of death," he told her. "What's really going on? Weren't you called in about some kind of sabotage?"

Nancy pursed her lips and looked over at him. "Yes," she said, "and we're not sure what the connection is. We do know the saboteur's been killed."

"Lampley?" Ned's handsome face was puzzled.

"No, no," Nancy said, taking a bite out of her toast. "His name was Pete Dawson. He was a handyman here."

Ned nodded slowly. "What about those tapes Frank mentioned?"

"Lampley's death happened on camera. There was a toast for the big donors, and his champagne was poisoned with cyanide. But whoever did it also wiped out the key footage, and the other camera wasn't focused on the action."

"So why are you checking it out again?" Ned asked. He cut into his omelet.

Nancy sighed. "Good question," she agreed. "Maybe we missed something. Even the best of us sometimes miss little things, especially if they're not what we're expecting to see."

"I don't understand."

"Well, we were all looking to see Lampley's glass doctored. That part's gone. But maybe there's something else, something the killer forgot to erase. I don't know. Joe thinks it's worth a try."

She pushed her breakfast away. "It's just a long shot. The police are convinced the culprit is Roseanne James. There's been a lot of evidence to back them up, but we all think she's innocent. Call it a gut feeling, but we've all got it. Joe's kind of in love with her, by the way." Nancy leaned back and smiled at him. "Maybe you'll see something we overlooked, Detective Nickerson."

"I'll do my best," he promised.

Nancy stroked his cheek. "Thanks for coming," Nancy murmured, gazing into his eyes. "I only wish you'd gotten here sooner."

Nancy caught sight of George striding briskly into the restaurant. "There you are!" George cried when she saw them. "We're all set to go downstairs. Hi, Ned! Good to see you." She and Ned gave each other a hug.

"Good to be here," Ned answered. "Nan, why don't we get these packed up to go? We can eat while we watch, can't we?"

"Good idea," Nancy replied, smiling at his eagerness.

George waited while Nancy and Ned had their breakfast wrapped. Then she led them down to the screening room. Frank, Joe, and Bess were waiting for them. Frank had decided Raven and Brad didn't need watching right then, and he needed everyone to look at the tapes.

Frank ran the tapes. First they looked at the main reel. They watched the waiter pouring the champagne, Roseanne and Brad singing in close-up, then Archer toasting and collapsing. Nancy concentrated so hard her head started to ache, but she couldn't see anything she'd missed before.

"Anybody?" Frank turned and asked them. They all shook their heads in unison. "All right," he went on, popping in another cassette. "Here are the outtakes. Look sharp."

The tape was a collection of random, seemingly unconnected shots. Raven had pieced together for them all the unused footage from three cameras.

One of the cameramen had panned the

tables during the last duet. For brief moments, the film showed parts of the dais, but Archer Lampley remained tantalizingly offscreen.

When the tape was over, Frank turned to them all again. "Well?" he asked.

They all looked at one another blankly. Ned seemed lost in thought. "Did you see something, Ned?" Nancy asked.

Ned answered slowly, "I'm not sure if I saw anything or not. Could you run it back a little, Frank?"

Frank obliged, and they found themselves looking at the footage of Ken's half of the dais. "Take it back to where the camera focuses on the head table," Ned instructed. "That's it. Now, look."

The waiter had already poured the final round. Brad and Roseanne were singing. The camera panned the dais, starting with Inez Ibarra, who looked bored, and Jack Treyford, who checked his watch. No wonder Raven hadn't used this segment for the final print.

The camera moved on to catch Ken Harrison, who was watching the singers intently. Then it panned back and refocused on another table.

"There!" Ned cried. "Did you see it?"

They all looked at him blankly. "Here, let me have that remote," he said, taking it from Frank's hand. He wound the tape back about ten seconds. "Look in the bottom left-hand corner of the screen."

Nancy looked where Ned was pointing, and could hardly believe her eyes. A man's hand, laden with rings, reached into the frame and swiped Ken Harrison's drink right out of the picture.

"I know that hand!" Frank cried. "It's Archer Lampley's! He wore rings on two fingers!"

The detectives all stared at one another in amazement.

"Archer must have finished his own drink in a hurry," Nancy said breathlessly. "Then, when he needed a full glass for the toast, he simply borrowed the nearest one—Ken's!"

"There's the connection you were looking for, Nancy," George said excitedly.

"I know. Now we've got the tie-in between the murder and the sabotage," Nancy agreed.

"Let's see it again," Frank suggested. He ran the tape back and played the section they were scrutinizing in slow motion.

"It's all there," Nancy murmured. "No question about it."

"Strange," Joe put in. "Ever since Archer was killed, we've wondered who wanted Lampley dead. But we've been asking ourselves the wrong question!"

"You've all been here awhile," Ned said calmly. "The question we should be asking is, who wants Ken Harrison dead?"

Chapter Twenty

NANCY GASPED. "You're right! Archer Lampley's murder was an accident, pure and simple."

"And reaching for Ken's glass cost Lampley his life," George added.

Frank nodded. "It looks like Ken Harrison was the intended victim all along. That would explain the sawed-off skis."

"I guess Pete outlived his usefulness," Nancy said grimly.

"Yeah," Joe agreed. "Or else the killer figured he was headed for the police."

"That makes sense, too," Nancy agreed soberly.

"Whew, this is spooky," Ned said, running a hand through his hair. "There have been two murders so far, but Ken Harrison is still walking around alive. Who knows what the killer will do next?"

Nancy leaned back in Raven's swivel chair and closed her eyes. Ned was right. The killer had not yet accomplished his mission. "I think we ought to get Ken out of sight for a while," she told her friends.

"Just what I was thinking." Frank nodded.

"Right," Joe added. "As far as I'm concerned, Ken is walking around with a big bull's-eye on his back."

"But if Ken is out of sight, then what happens?" Ned wanted to know. "Are we back to square one?"

"Not quite," Nancy answered him. "I'm beginning to get a clearer picture of things now. Remember Ken telling us how Jack Treyford has been after him to sell Mount Mirage to Treyford Industries?"

"Yes," George said. The others nodded.

"Well, I think we should definitely take Treyford up on his party invitation tonight. There's a lot we still don't know about him."

"You're right, Nancy," Frank said slowly. "And his party is the perfect place to find out just what kind of person Jack Treyford is—and how far he'd go to have Mount Mirage."

* * *

"Hello. May I take your coats?" The uniformed maid opened Treyford's door with a pleasant smile.

"Thanks," Ned said, turning to Nancy to help her with her jacket.

"Follow me, please," the maid said after she had collected their coats. She led them through a wood-paneled corridor to an immense sunken living room.

It was just past sunset. Nancy looked through the windows at the far end of the room and saw the sky beginning to darken. As she watched, the first twinkling stars came out.

"Nice place," Ned said.

"Not bad," Nancy returned, smiling as she looked around. Treyford's villa was more than nice, it was sumptuous. In the center of the room was a round fireplace, visible from any direction. The walls were richly decorated with original art, lit from above. One wall had shelves displaying various objects and treasures.

"Would you care for some fruit punch?" A waiter approached them, bearing a tray of fine crystal stemware.

"Thanks," Nancy said, helping herself to a glass.

Ned nodded his thanks and took a glass for himself. "Looks like we're early."

There were only about a half-dozen guests at the party so far. Nancy recognized most of the early arrivals as guests from the lodge. She and Ned nodded pleasantly to them as they sipped their punch. Treyford was nowhere in sight.

In the corner, a chamber trio began a light Mozart piece. Nancy felt a tap on her shoulder. She spun around and saw Frank. With him were Joe, Bess, and George.

"Hi!" Nancy cried. "Where's Brad?"

Bess pouted. "He's coming by snowmobile with Raven. He said they had some business to discuss. But he also said he'd see me here," she added, a note of forlorn hope in her voice.

"The place is really filling up now," Ned said. The level of conversation around them increased in volume. As the trio played in the background, guests began mingling and chatting.

"Hello, everybody!" Jack Treyford appeared to be in high spirits as he stepped down into the living room. Inez Ibarra was next to him, looking glamorous in an off-the-shoulder white satin dress.

Laughing, Treyford helped himself to a glass of punch from a passing tray. "No poison in this!" he quipped, downing the punch.

Some of the guests tittered uncomfortably at Treyford's joke.

Brad MacDougal and Raven Maxwell arrived. To Nancy's surprise, Brad was dressed in a business suit. As for Raven, she was wearing a burgundy silk dress.

"Hi," Raven said softly as she and Brad stepped into the room, holding hands.

Nancy glanced quickly at Bess. Her cheeks had flushed a deep shade of pink.

"Come on, Joe," Bess muttered, yanking his arm. "Let's see if they have any food here."

Joe smiled. "How can I resist such a gracious invitation?" he replied, following her to the buffet table.

"I think I'll take a look around," Frank said. "Want to come, George?"

"Sure," George answered, following him.

"Hello there, folks!" Turning, Nancy saw Chester and Pearl Peabody. Chester was wearing his usual friendly grin, but Pearl looked upset.

"I saw your friends skiing to the party," Chester said. "Ken let us borrow a snowmobile. I offered him a lift, but he said he couldn't come tonight. He wanted to catch up on some paperwork."

Nancy was glad to hear Ken was following their advice and laying low. He probably wouldn't have come to this party, anyway, she reflected.

"Well, I don't know why we're at a party, with all the awful things that have happened," Pearl confessed, a worried look in her eye. "Some people are saying everything's fine now that Roseanne James has been taken into custody, but I just can't believe that girl is a killer. I feel sick at heart about her being arrested."

"Pearl's a big fan," Chester explained. "She loved Jocelyn James, too. She didn't eat for three days when Jocelyn died. Honey," he said, looking her straight in the eye, "you've got to ease up and enjoy your own life. That's my philosophy. Now come on, let's check out that food table." Pulling his wife gently by the elbow, he walked away.

Treyford was standing behind Nancy and Ned, speaking to the head of Worldwide Children's Charities. A small group had gathered to listen.

"I've always gotten my way in business because I'm always prepared. That's all it takes—a little homework," Treyford said, glancing at Inez Ibarra, who was posed next to him.

"For instance, I always have two plans," Treyford went on. "Sometimes three or four. That way, if Plan A goes wrong, I've got somewhere to go. Plan B, Plan C, they're the ones you wind up using half the time, anyway."

Nancy turned to study him, trying to see beneath the urbane surface of the man. Jack Treyford was an extremely wealthy man—yet he seemed far from happy or satisfied.

"Nancy, Ned, could you come over here a second?" George's voice was a soft whisper.

They followed her to the other side of the room. Frank stood there, pretending to look at some of the leather-bound books on display.

"What's up?" Ned asked.

Still holding the book, Frank pointed to one of the pages. "Isn't this interesting? It's a Currier and Ives print," he said in a normal voice. Then, checking around to make sure no one was listening, he added, "Check out that plaque on the third shelf."

Nancy walked over to the shelf. The plaque read, "To Jack Treyford, Inventor of Treyford Cable, a Quantum Advance in Engineering." A knot of purplish cable was mounted beneath the dedication.

Nancy remembered where she'd seen wire like that before—on Ken's desk that first day they'd arrived at Mount Mirage. It was the same wire that had been used to stall the ski lift!

Chapter Twenty-One

FRANK WAS SMILING NOW. "When I saw the wire, it put my mind in motion," he said softly. "First someone tries to run Ken out of business by sabotaging things. It doesn't work. So he tries something else."

Nancy's blue eyes lit up. "That's Treyford all over!" she whispered.

"We know he's been trying to buy this place for a long time, and Ken wouldn't sell," Frank went on. "Getting Mount Mirage for himself could be his motive."

"Treyford has been up here lots of times," Nancy added. "He would know Pete Dawson."

"Except his plan with Pete didn't work," Frank said. "So he tried a second plan—murdering Ken!"

"Hold on, guys," George broke in. "Mount Mirage is peanuts to a guy like Treyford. He could have any ski resort he wanted. Why this one?"

Nancy bit her lip. "Good question. We know Treyford's been criticizing the way Ken runs Mount Mirage. He might want to show the world he can run the resort better. But he'd have to be crazy to *kill* for that reason."

"He's very intense and driven," George observed. "Maybe too much. He could be unbalanced."

"Bess looks upset," Ned said suddenly.

Nancy looked up and saw Joe and Bess walking toward them. "Hi, guys," Bess said, practically in tears. "Enjoying the party?"

"It's very interesting," Frank said with a gleam in his brown eyes. "Come on, Joe. Let's take a walk. We found a couple of things you should know about."

"I think Brad's in love with Raven," Bess announced miserably after Joe and Frank had walked off. "They're totally wrapped up in each other."

"I'm sorry, Bess. I know how much you liked him," Nancy told her friend sympathetically.

George put a comforting arm around her

cousin. "Come on," she said, leading Bess away. "Tell me all about it."

With a little wave to Nancy, George guided Bess to a sofa. Good old George. She always knew what to do.

Nancy stood next to Ned, looking across the large room at Treyford. She was acting her part as a casual party guest, but inside, her detective instincts were spinning.

"He's the one, Ned. He's got to be," she murmured.

"You need evidence," Ned told her, looking concerned. "Any ideas?"

"Not yet," she said with a sigh.

"The motive's not all there, either," he reminded her. "Why this place? Why not buy another ski resort?"

"You're right," she agreed. They glanced at their host, who was still holding court across the room. He had a dead expression in his eyes, and the smirk of a shark about to devour its prey on his lips.

As he talked, Treyford gestured expansively. The gold of his cuff links winked at Nancy.

"Gold," she said out loud.

"What about it?" Ned asked.

Frank and Joe were headed their way. The musicians had just finished a piece. Nancy beckoned the brothers closer, then waited for the music to start again.

"About the motive," she said softly when the next piece began. "What if it's gold he's after? Pete was a gold miner, right? What if Pete actually did find gold and showed it to Treyford? That would have gotten him excited. Maybe even excited enough to commit murder!"

Frank and Joe were looking at her intently.

"He's a greedy guy, that's for sure," Frank said. "Everything you're saying feels right, but we still need hard evidence."

Joe's eyes were burning with indignation. "Well, we better get it, because no way am I going to sit back and let Roseanne James be destroyed for a crime somebody else committed!" he said hotly.

"What about Inez Ibarra? Where does she fit in?" Ned asked.

Nancy glanced across the room again. Inez was holding Treyford's arm, gazing up at him adoringly. "I think Inez is just part of his idea of the perfect image," Nancy said. "He'd never confide in her."

"So." Joe's tone of voice was decisive. "What do we do?"

Nancy took a deep breath. "I have an idea. We could try a bluff," she began. "Make him think we have proof. But we'll need a diversion, and we've got to make sure the exits are covered. I'll take care of the bluff, unless someone else wants the job."

"Diversion and guard are just my speed," Joe said with a smile.

"Nancy, bluffing can be dangerous." Ned wasn't crazy about the idea, Nancy could tell. "What happens if he doesn't fall for it?"

"But, Ned," Frank said with a wry grin, "Nancy's a very convincing person."

"I don't want her to get in trouble, that's all," Ned protested.

"Me, neither," Frank said. "But I think Treyford will fall for a bluff. He's ready. Look at him, he's wound up like a coil."

"Ned, I don't see any other way. Do you?" Nancy asked, touching his arm.

"What kind of a bluff are you thinking of?" Ned said finally. "And where do you want me?"

"I want you at the main exit. As for the bluff, I'll play it by ear. Wish me luck."

Ned shook his head in mock disapproval. "Being your boyfriend puts gray hairs on my head, you know that?"

"Thanks, Ned," she said, standing on tiptoe to give him a kiss.

"That leaves you and me for the diversion," Frank told Joe. "Oh, boy, I'm going to love this. How long do you need, Nancy?"

"Just three or four minutes. When you see me walk over to Inez, I'll be ready."

"Should I alert Bess and George?" Ned offered.

"Good idea," Nancy told him. "They can stand guard, too."

"We'll start in two minutes then," Frank said, glancing at his watch.

As Joe and Frank sauntered past the musicians, Nancy slipped over to a wall unit across the room. She lingered there, casting her glance around, waiting for Frank and Joe to get ready.

The two minutes passed. Suddenly Frank's voice echoed across the room. "I'm telling you, Joe, she's bad news!" he shouted loudly.

Joe's face tightened with rage. "Leave her out of this!" he demanded.

"The police are convinced she did it," Frank taunted.

"Roseanne James is a beautiful human being. Don't talk about her that way. Or I'll—"

"You'll what?"

"I'll punch your lights out!"

"Just try!" Frank shouted.

The challenge was too much for Joe. With one convincing stage punch, the fight was on.

George and Bess shrieked and begged anyone who'd listen to break up the fight. Brad MacDougal rushed over to the Hardy brothers and tried to pull Joe away from Frank.

While the guests watched in stunned amazement, Nancy reached down and riffled through Treyford's collection of videotapes.

Deftly, she pulled one from the shelf and

peeled off the label. Then she slipped the unmarked tape into her handbag.

"Sorry," Joe was saying as he let Brad cool him off. "I just can't stand it when he puts her down."

Inez Ibarra looked totally shocked. She obviously wasn't used to fistfights at the parties she attended.

"If you can't conduct yourselves like gentlemen, I suggest you leave!" Treyford's voice was quivering with anger. "Mary, get their jackets, please."

Frank and Joe took their positions at two separate exits. Ned was covering the door to the kitchen.

Nancy approached Inez Ibarra. "I have a videotape I'd like to play," she told the model. "I think a lot of the guests will enjoy it. It's footage of the 'High Life' documentary," Nancy explained in a loud voice.

The glamorous model looked puzzled but seemed to welcome the change of pace.

"It will certainly be better than the performance we just saw," she remarked as she opened a cabinet to reveal a large-screen TV and a VCR.

"Hello, attention everybody!" Nancy called out. "Attention, please!" The room grew quiet, and all eyes turned her way.

Nancy flashed the guests a dazzling smile. "I have a tape I'd like to share with you," she said. "It's been a difficult time for many of us here at Mount Mirage. We came together for a great cause, Worldwide Children's Charities. But along the way, two people lost their lives, and the rest of us have been in danger."

Nancy looked out at the puzzled faces of the guests. Treyford was looking distinctly uncomfortable.

"I don't mean to frighten anyone, but Roseanne James is not guilty. The murderer is here among us—right now."

As Nancy expected, the party guests began buzzing. Some cast wary glances at their neighbors.

"You see, Roseanne has been set up to take the rap. Archer Lampley's death was an accident. The murderer really meant to kill Ken Harrison."

Nancy looked over at Treyford again. His eyes had narrowed, and he was looking at her with barely concealed fury.

"Archer grabbed Ken's drink for the toast and drank poison that was meant for Ken." The guests were buzzing now. Nancy continued, "Now, there were several cameras at the toast that night. The killer erased vital evidence on one of the tapes, but we found another. It shows the murderer putting cyanide in Ken's glass."

Her heart pounding in her chest, Nancy

reached for the VCR, pressed the Eject button, and inserted the tape she was holding.

"You'll see the killer now, doctoring Ken's drink." She glanced at Treyford again, but he didn't meet her eyes. He had to bite! she thought. If he didn't, she'd look like a fool and Roseanne would go to jail. Now was the time.

She took a deep breath, then, slowly, reached for the Play button.

Chapter Twenty-Two

"HOLD IT RIGHT THERE!" Treyford shouted. He stormed over to the VCR and pressed the Eject button. "Thank you," he said sarcastically. Then he tossed the tape into the fire.

Nancy stared at him, cool as ice. "As you must have guessed, Mr. Treyford, I've already had a copy made. It's being delivered to the police at this very moment."

"That will do, Ms. Drew," said Treyford. He reached into his pocket and pulled out a small glass tube. "I happen to have on me a vial of highly explosive liquid. I wouldn't want to use it, but if I must, I will not hesitate. As it is, I'm afraid I shall have to make other arrangements for my future."

"Plan C?" Nancy asked, playing for time. Out of the corner of her eye she saw Frank, Joe, and Ned inching forward, waiting for an opportunity. She hoped they'd be careful. Treyford's little vial might be the end of them all.

"If you like, Plan C," Treyford said, giving her a brisk nod. "I congratulate you. You and your friends are very resourceful. But I have resources, too."

Nancy shook her head in amazement. "You're one of the most brazen criminals I've ever seen," she told him. "Do you really think you can get away with murder, just because you're Jack Treyford?"

"I don't think, young lady, I *know*. There are plenty of governments in this world that will be happy to shelter me and my resources. Inez, my dear, I'm sorry it worked out this way. You understand, I couldn't possibly let you know what was happening."

Inez was too stunned to talk. She leaned back, supporting herself against the wall.

Treyford drew a remote-control device from a pocket of his jacket. He pushed a button and Nancy heard a click as all the doors were automatically locked. Security shades dropped, sealing off all the windows. Frank,

Joe, and Ned frantically ran to the doors and pulled at them. It was useless. They were trapped.

As Treyford watched them, he let out a vicious laugh. Then he moved to one edge of the Oriental carpet and lifted it up. Underneath was a trapdoor.

The mine shaft! Nancy remembered the shaft went off in two directions from under Pete Dawson's shack. So it ran under Treyford's villa, too!

"I'll be leaving all of you now." Treyford smiled snidely. "I'm sure you'll be rescued soon enough."

In a flash he was gone. The trapdoor slammed down, and a sharp click indicated that it had been bolted from below. Just like Treyford, Nancy thought, to have a built-in escape hatch.

"Unbelievable!" Joe cried, trying without success to pull up the door. Other guests were banging on the doors and windows, yelling for help.

"George! Bess! Call the police!" Nancy shouted, as she bent down to pry at the trapdoor with Joe.

Frank stood in the middle of the room in stunned amazement. "There's got to be a way out of here," he murmured.

But the trapdoor wouldn't budge, even when Joe tried to jimmy the lock.

"Um, excuse me, but I, um, I might be able to help you folks." It was Chester L. Peabody, holding in his hands what looked like some sort of a pencil.

"I call this a laser etch. It's a sculptor's tool, actually, which I recently developed," he explained. "You see, it's got a miniature laser, and it burns through whatever material you're working on, so you can—"

"So we can burn our way out of here!" Joe Hardy cried exultantly.

"Quit explaining what it does, and show us how it works, Chester!" Frank urged him.

Chester bent down to start on the trapdoor, but Nancy stopped him. "No, the front door!" she urged. "It'll be faster!"

Chester went up to the door and etched his way through the lock. The process could only have taken five minutes, but it seemed like five hours to Nancy. With every passing second, Jack Treyford was getting farther and farther away!

"Give it a push now, and I think it'll give," Chester said. He backed away from the door.

Ned tried first but didn't have any luck. The door wouldn't budge.

"Here!" Frank shouted, pointing to a long bench. "Let's use this."

Frank, Ned, and Joe picked up the bench and rammed the door with it. With a sharp bang, the door flew open.

"Come on, guys!" Frank cried. "Let's go!"

Nancy, Bess, and George rushed out after Frank, Joe, and Ned into the night air. "The snowmobiles!" Nancy called out, running toward where the guests had parked. "Come on!"

She and Ned hopped on one snowmobile, while Frank and Joe grabbed another.

"Listen!" Frank shouted. "Hear the motor noise? Treyford's down by the snowmobile lot!"

Nancy could just make out the noise. Treyford was already below the resort, on his way down the mountain and into town.

"After him!" Frank gunned his motor, and Nancy did the same. She followed Frank down the dark hillside as he skillfully dodged trees, boulders, and steep ravines. The sound of Treyford's motor grew louder, but he was still far ahead.

Then, abruptly, Frank stopped. Nancy pulled up alongside. "If we go that way," Frank said breathlessly, pointing down a particularly steep slope, "we can make up some distance. Are you up for it?"

Nancy nodded. There was no turning back now.

"Hold on tight!" she told Ned.

They plunged downward, flying over pockets and skidding across sheets of ice. Swerving wildly to miss trees that seemed to fly into their path, Nancy and Frank sped down the mountain. Then, just as they were halfway down, Nancy lost track of Treyford. She slowed the snowmobile. Frank must have had the same problem because he stopped completely.

"He seems to know just where he's going," Frank said as Nancy pulled up next to him by a clump of trees. "He must have mapped out his getaway beforehand, just in case."

"Just like him. Where is he now?" Nancy wondered.

The buzz of a distant motor gave her the answer. Treyford sounded as if he were a few hundred yards ahead. Nancy gunned her engine and sped off, the roar of Frank's engine close behind.

They were catching up to Treyford now. The sound of his snowmobile grew louder and louder. Nancy looked around for the Hardys when she had a second in the clear, but they had disappeared!

"I hope they didn't wipe out," she shouted to Ned.

Ned nodded. "Me, too. But let's worry about Treyford first. We've almost got him."

Ned was right. Treyford's snowmobile was only about twenty yards ahead now. Nancy could see his panicked face as he turned back to look at his pursuers.

"I'm going to jump him!" Ned shouted as

she gunned the engine again and managed to pull up alongside the rear of Treyford's snowmobile.

With a loud yell, Ned jumped. The force nearly sent Nancy's vehicle out of control. But, turning to look, she saw Ned had landed squarely on Treyford's back. The surprised killer struggled wildly, trying to loosen Ned's grip around his neck. Nancy watched in alarm as he broke the grip of Ned's right hand. With his left hand, Ned held on to Treyford's coat.

It was all Nancy could do to keep pace with the other snowmobile. Treyford, with Ned on his back, had allowed his vehicle to get out of control and was struggling to steer clear of hazards.

She was beginning to formulate a plan, when suddenly the Hardys reappeared. They seemed to come from out of nowhere on Treyford's right. With a startled yell, Treyford veered away from them and right in front of Nancy's snowmobile.

Nancy shrieked and pulled her vehicle to the left at the very last second.

Frank had outflanked Treyford, catching him completely unaware. Nancy looked on in horror as Treyford's vehicle headed toward the edge of a steep ravine.

"Ned! Jump!" Nancy screamed over the roar of the motors.

Ned let go of Treyford's coat and hopped off,

landing in a huge snowdrift. Nancy and Frank both braked their snowmobiles, whipping around in opposite directions to avoid going over the edge.

Treyford's vehicle swung wildly out of control. He seemed to be trying to brake, but without any luck. He sped closer and closer to the ravine. Helpless, Nancy watched in horror as Treyford's snowmobile went flying over the edge!

Chapter Twenty-Three

"We'll take care of him," Frank shouted, pointing to where Treyford had landed. "You make sure Ned's okay."

"Thanks, Frank." Nancy swiftly rode back to where Ned had landed. He was digging his way out of the snowbank.

"Ned! Are you okay?" she cried.

"I think so," he said, dusting himself off. "The snow's pretty soft, thank goodness."

"Oh, Ned!" Nancy said breathily, throwing herself into his arms and hugging him tightly.

"Next time, you do the jumping, okay?" he said with a laugh. "Hey, did we get our man?"

"I think we did." Nancy nodded soberly. "But I'm not sure if he's dead or alive."

They rode over to where the Hardys' vehicle was parked, at the edge of the ravine. Looking over, Nancy saw Joe and Frank by the wreck of Treyford's snowmobile. They were rolling it over, trying to get it off him.

"He's alive!" Joe shouted up at them. "But just barely."

Frank scrambled up and dusted himself off. "If there'd been much fuel in the tank, it would have exploded on top of him. He's incredibly lucky."

"I don't know," Nancy replied. "I have a feeling Jack Treyford's luck has just run out."

When Nancy, Bess, and George came down to the lobby early the next morning, they noticed that bright film lights had been set up by the huge fireplace.

"What's going on?" Nancy wondered.

Stepping closer, she saw Raven Maxwell busily giving interviews to all three network news teams at once!

"I don't want you all to think," she was saying, "that I solved this case all on my own. It's true, I did come up with the key piece of evidence, the videotape, but the unsung hero of the case is really my client, Brad MacDougal. Brad was truly brilliant."

"Can you believe this?" Bess was aghast. "How can she lie like that? Nobody's going to believe her."

George laughed. "They'll believe her, all right. She's first on the air with the story. Anything anyone else says now will be looked on as publicity grabbing. See how much I learned from Raven in just two days, Nancy?"

Nancy nodded. "I don't care so much about the credit," she said sincerely. "I'm just glad Treyford is taken care of."

Bess grimaced as Raven brought Brad up to the mikes and cameras. She was hugging his arm tightly and batting her eyelashes at him. Brad and Raven looked for all the world like America's crown couple.

"I can't stand it," Bess cried, gritting her teeth. "Get me out of here before I throw up."

"Take it easy, Bess," George comforted her. "There'll be other rock stars."

Bess stared at the couple in the spotlight and snorted derisively. "Boy, am I ever glad I gave *him* the brush."

"What?" George cried. "Who gave whom the brush? Bess, are you rewriting history, too? It's bad enough Raven's doing it."

"'The winners write the history books,'" Nancy quoted with a wry smile. "I forget who said that."

Bess scowled. "Oh, well. At least I can say I knew the real Brad MacDougal."

George and Nancy burst into appreciative laughter. Bess Marvin truly was a survivor!

Ken Harrison walked up to them. "I want to thank you girls for the great job you did," he said, beaming. "You and the Hardys saved me and Mount Mirage from complete disaster. With all the publicity of Treyford being captured, I think we've got a winner on our hands again. You know, it's ironic. When you suggested I go into hiding, I was almost ready to give it up, to go see Treyford and tell him I'd sell him the place."

Frank and Ned came down the main stairs and walked over to them. "Hi, everyone!" Frank said.

"Good morning, all," Ned echoed, planting a kiss on Nancy's cheek.

"Where's Joe?" Bess asked. "Still sleeping?"

"Not a chance. He's on the phone with Roseanne. They let her out of jail this morning, but I don't think she's coming back to Mount Mirage. Joe's pretty upset."

"Wow. I don't blame him." Nancy was concerned. "Why isn't she coming? Doesn't she want to see him anymore?"

Frank shrugged. "I only heard Joe's end of the conversation, but it sounded like she wanted a rest from everything. She's starting a world tour in two weeks. She was saying she'd write to him and call him when she got back in August."

"August? That's months from now!" George said.

"Poor Joe! He must be devastated!" Bess sympathized. "Can't he join her on the world tour or something?"

"Uh-uh," Frank said, shaking his head. "We've already got two cases lined up. But don't worry about Joe; work's the best therapy for him."

"All the same," Bess replied, "he could probably use some company right now. I'll go check on him." She took a quick look in her compact and ran off up the stairs. "See you in a few!" she called as she disappeared.

Frank turned to Nancy with a confused look on his face. "Nancy, there's just one thing I want to clear up," he said. "It's about Treyford's motive. Do you really think he was after gold?"

"Gold? Somebody say gold?" Chester L. Peabody, with Pearl on his arm, was stepping up to them. "Oh, Mr. Harrison, are you going to be surprised. Talk about gold!"

Peabody held up a small gauge in his hand. "This is a handy-dandy little prospecting tool I invented two years ago for my cousin Ernest, who's a panner up in Alaska. It's a gold meter. I took it out back, dug a little hole, and this thing started going crazy! Yes, sir! There's gold under this mountain. Lots of it. You, sir, are going to be a very rich man."

Ken looked stunned. He took the meter in his hands, looked at it for a moment, then handed it back to its inventor. "Thanks, Mr. Peabody," he said softly. "But I'm already rich enough. Mount Mirage will never be stripped for mines of any sort. Not while I own it."

He put his arms around Nancy and Frank. "But really," he said out loud. "Gold! On my mountain! Can you believe it?"

"Oh, believe it, Mr. Harrison," Chester L. Peabody said with a loud guffaw. "Stranger things have happened. Look at me," he added, indicating his squat, portly figure. "Would you believe I won twenty million dollars in a lottery?"